EDUCATION: DOMESTICATION

MIDDLE SCHOOL MAYHEM BOOK TEN

C.T. WALSH

FARCICAL PRESS

COVER CREDITS

Cover design by Books Covered
Cover photographs © Shutterstock
Cover illustrations by Maeve Norton

For my Family

Thank you for all of your support

1

You ever have someone tell you to grow up? I get that all the time. Perhaps I'm a bit immature, so maybe I get it more than you, but what's wrong with that? Everybody walks around, saying, "Oh, he's so mature" (they're not talking about me, as you already know), like that means something. What they're really saying is, "Oh, he's a no-fun doofus." At least, that's what I think.

Why do they want us kids to grow up so fast? All the adults I know complain every day about being old. "My legs are tired. My back aches. My butt is too wrinkly. My memory is...what was I talking about again?" Complaints. Complaints. Complaints. They get butt lifts, face lifts, and a whole host of other surgeries to fix old, sagging stuff. And then they go and take away our recess, but we find out all they want to do is retire so they can play. They all want to be young again, but everybody else needs to grow up. It's just not right.

My parents are always telling me that school was so much tougher when they were kids. Like I really believe them that they had to walk to school barefoot in the snow during the apocalypse. I bet they never got duct taped to the wall. Or the floor. Or to Barney "Barn Door" Herbert, for that matter. It's a long story. Just know that duct tape is the new spit ball in this generation and it's a doozy. And so is the rest of this story.

Which brings me to my point. Home economics and health. The dreaded eighth-grade subject my friends and I had to endure to graduate middle school. My older sister, Leighton, went through it and almost dropped out of school and became a nun. She wouldn't have been a very good nun, but that's not the point.

Apparently, the intent of home economics and health was to help tame and domesticate the wild middle school population and help us mature, as we finish out our final year before heading to high school. We're kids for God's sake. We don't need to be tamed or domesticated. Middle school isn't a zoo. True, there's mayhem, but we're a lot more civilized than zoo animals. Yeah, we might blow off some steam by duct taping a peer to the wall or drawing a mustache on a sleeping student, but we don't bite or eat each other when we're angry. Well, Amanda Gluskin might, but why should all of us have to endure the school's attempt at domestication when only a few kids can't function normally in society?

This story started off innocently enough, as they always do. I was sitting in my kitchen and eating some mac 'n cheese that my mother had made for me. It was a big day. As soon as I finished eating, I was heading over to my girl-friend's house. Sophie and I were going to babysit her little cousin while her aunt and uncle were in town, so the adults could go out for dinner. I was looking forward to it, but I was also a little nervous. The last time I had been over her house, the fire department was required to remove me from the doggie door. It's a long story. You may have heard it before. It was a disaster. The whole town hated me because we ran out of butter for a week after I used up the town's supply to extract me. I smelled like movie popcorn for quite a few weeks after that, too. I don't know why everyone was so upset. It wasn't like it was bacon or anything. I'm pretty certain Amazon can ship a vat of butter in like six seconds, but what do I know? I'm only a middle school kid taking high school science classes.

Anyway, Sophie's parents were trusting me, and I wasn't sure I would make it through without some mayhem ensuing. I tended to attract it. And this time, there would be a baby involved. Sophie assured me her cousin was a piece of cake to watch, but the only thing I was good at watching was Netflix.

My mom walked in, as I was scarfing down an oversized bite of my food. "Would it kill you and your brother to clean up after yourselves? There's dirty laundry everywhere. There's literally dirty underwear hanging from the chandelier," she said, angrily.

I gulped my food down and answered, "If it's my Spiderman underwear, it's not my fault. They just like to hang upside down."

"I'm serious, Austin. I'm not the maid. You guys need to do a better job of keeping things neat around here."

"Sorry, Mom. I'll talk to my underwear."

My mother shook her head and then looked at her watch and gasped. "Austin, you have to hurry up. You don't want to be late," she said, out of breath. Everybody knew Sophie was out of my league and that my life would crumble to pieces without her, so the whole family was on egg shells any time there was a chance she could be disappointed.

My mother leaned on the chair next to mine, breathing deeply, and looking pale. It seemed like she was overreacting a bit, though.

"She's not gonna dump me if we're late." I stared at her for a second. "Are you okay?" I asked.

"I'm not feeling well," she said. "But I'll be okay."

She would not be okay. And neither would my mac 'n cheese. Without warning, my mother heaved and then hurled with a "Huwullah!" The force of the heave caused her to double over, her mouth lining up with my dinner bowl. Not a whole lot came out, but what did was a less-than-appetizing topping on my previously-magnificent mac.

"Mom! What the heck?" It was not a great reaction, but that's what you get for messing with my mac. "I mean, ummm, are you okay?"

"I'm sorry," she said, wiping her mouth, as she walked

slowly over to the sink. "My stomach has been queasy all day."

I looked down at my bowl of mac, cheese, and hurl and pushed it toward the center of the table. I was no longer hungry for some reason.

"I'm just going to lie down," my mother said, walking into the den. "Sorry about your dinner. I'll give you money to order a pizza at Sophie's."

"Okay. Don't worry about it. I'll get it from Dad. Can I get you anything?" I know, what a great son, right?

"No, I'll be fine."

My annoying brother, Derek, walked into the kitchen from the outside door that opened to the backyard. He lumbered over to the table. My back was to him, as I looked in at my mom resting on the couch.

"You gonna eat the rest of this?" Derek asked.

"No," I said, mindlessly. And then his question registered. I turned around quickly, but it was too late.

My former fork was leaving Derek's mouth, a huge bite of mac, cheese, and hurl already mashing in his mouth. My face dropped. And so did my stomach. Not because it was gross. It was, but it was more so because of what it could mean for the rest of my body. If Derek found out I let him eat puke, he would pummel me. Even though we were in the same grade, he was eleven months older than me. Plus, he got the sports genes and the family butt chin while I got the brains and a rather non-descript chin.

"What?" he asked, annoyed.

"Nothing." I knew it was too late to save Derek. But I could still save myself. "It's really good," I said. "Eat up." Sorry, but he deserved it. If you haven't heard any of my other stories, you might not understand, but trust me. You will.

"It's a little wetter than normal, but it's still so good. Might be Mom's best batch," Derek said, shrugging.

"Could be. Well, enjoy! Gotta run." I headed out of the room as quickly as I could, hoping that my mother would never find out about the whole fiasco, and even more so, Derek.

I found my dad outside. He was just finishing up some sort of meeting with a guy about the house. He looked at me and nodded. "Be right there, bud."

I hopped into the car and watched the front door like a hawk, hoping Derek wouldn't burst out like a wild animal, ready to hunt me down. I locked the doors just in case.

As my dad approached, I checked to make sure Derek was still inside the house, and then unlocked the doors. My dad slipped into the car and plopped down beside me.

"All good?" my Dad asked.

"As good as ever," I responded, remembering Derek's mouthful of hurl in slow motion. "Who was that dude?"

"Ah, just a contractor. I don't have time to fix a few things around the house, so I'm just gonna get a quote. You ready for your first babysitting gig?"

"Not sure. I guess we'll see."

"Yeah, I'm sure the baby's parents would be excited to hear that," he said, laughing. The car revved to life and we took off down the road.

I checked the rear-view mirror for Derek just in case. He was the fastest kid in school and if he knew he had eaten Mom's puke, he'd probably be able to catch us.

The coast was clear. I exhaled, as we navigated the local traffic en route to Sophie's house. After a few minutes, we pulled up to her house. I hadn't been there too many times. I was a little bit nervous. Sure, the baby added some concern, but I was pretty sure her dad didn't like me that much. I had once camped out on their lawn, refusing to leave until Sophie talked to me, and then there was the doggie door, butter, fire department debacle.

"Mom said you would give me money for pizza," I said, holding my hand out.

"What happened to the mac 'n cheese?"

"There were...complications."

"Complications?" he asked, handing me a twenty.

"Derek ate it." It was the truth. Not the whole truth, but I couldn't start spreading the puke story.

"Good luck."

"Thanks," I said, stepping out of the car. I closed the door, took a deep breath, and headed toward Sophie's house, where certain doom awaited.

2

———————

The door opened slowly, revealing a tiny, smiling face peering out at me. The little girl had brown, uneven pig tails on the sides of her head. The door opened the rest of the way. Sophie stood there, also with a smile, holding the little girl.

"Come in," Sophie said with a head nod.

I opened the door and entered.

"Meet my cousin, Maddie."

"Hi, Maddie," I said, holding out my hand for a shake.

She thrust her fist forward to my finger tips for a fist bump and then pulled it back with explosion-like sound effects. "Boom, baby," she said, sweetly.

Sophie laughed while I exhaled, realizing she was kind of cool, and that there was a good chance we would have a lot of fun and not burn the house down. The last thing I needed was another visit from the fire department at Sophie's house.

"Maddie, this is Austin."

"Authtin."

"Close enough," I smiled, while I followed Sophie and Maddie into the living room.

We were met by Sophie's parents and her aunt and uncle.

"Hi, Austin," Sophie's mom said with a smile. "This is my sister and brother-in-law, Maddie's parents."

I waved and said, "It's nice to meet you." I shook hands with both of them. I smiled and held out my hand, as I looked up at Sophie's dad. "Good to see you, Mr. Rodriguez."

Mr. Rodriguez eyed me up and down and then shook my hand. "Austin," he said, simply. "What are your qualifications to oversee the care of my beautiful niece?"

I wasn't prepared for the question. Nor was I all that prepared for the job. "Umm, well, I was a baby once, so...I know what it's like from their perspective. I also have a very immature brother."

"How old is he?" Sophie's mother asked.

"Thirteen."

Everyone laughed. Crisis averted.

"Well, we're in a rush. Sophie, you know where all her stuff is. Dinner is made. It just needs to be heated up. Call my cell if you need anything," Sophie's mom said, as the adults headed toward the front door.

"Bye, bye, sweetie," Aunt Carol said.

The door closed behind them, essentially setting off a firestorm. No, we didn't need the fire department, but who knows? Maybe they could have helped. Maddie burst into tears and shrieked at the top of her lungs, "Momma! Momma! Don't go!"

"It's okay, sweetie," Sophie said, cheerily.

I wanted to put my fingers in my ears and run out the

back door, but I figured that wouldn't be overly helpful to Sophie. In the absence of that, I didn't know what to do.

"Do you want your binky?" Sophie asked, a little less cheerily.

"No!"

Sophie bounced Maddie up and down in her arms. "Do you want to eat your dinner? Yummy pasta."

"No!" Maddie crossed her arms and seemingly tried to burn Sophie to a crisp with her eyes. Thankfully, Maddie wasn't super human.

"Austin, do something," Sophie said, now nearing panic levels.

"I don't know what to do."

"Sing a song or dance. Break a lamp over your head. Whatever you have to do," Sophie said.

"That's a little extreme. I'll start with a song." I tapped my chin for a moment and then bust out into a song I wrote for my band, Mayhem Mad Men. "6 A.M. wakeup. The halls are filled with too much body spray, perfume and makeup! I gotta claw through the fumes just to get to the bathroom."

"Makeup! Makeup!" Maddie yelled, her tears disappearing into thin air.

Sophie bit her lip, bracing for another explosion. "You can't have makeup, Maddie."

"On him!" Maddie yelled, pointing to me. "Makeup on Authtin!"

"Oh, no. That's not gonna happen."

Maddie's eyes exploded with tears like a water balloon popped and she screamed so loud and with every ounce of her body, I saw every tooth she had and even what she ate yesterday.

Sophie looked at me, her eyes pleading.

"Okay, Maddie. Makeup," I said, unenthused.

"Yay!" Sophie cheered.

Maddie stopped crying abruptly and clapped. "Makeup on Authtin!"

I sat down on the couch, accepting my fate, as Sophie disappeared with Maddie, and then returned with a floral makeup bag.

"Pick your poison," she said with a smile, holding the bag open for me to see all of the items that would be smeared all over my face.

"Maybe just a little cover up?" I said, disgusted with myself.

"Whipthtick!" Maddie yelled. "Whipthtick!"

I was about to say no, but Sophie grabbed the lipstick as quickly as she could and handed it to Maddie. I couldn't resist when Maddie's eyes lit up. She was so happy, and I couldn't handle any more crying. I was on the verge of a nervous breakdown or something.

Apparently, two-year olds aren't well-developed in the area of motor control. Lipstick was more like facestick. Maddie stuck her tongue out, as she concentrated on turning me into a clown.

"It looks good on you," Sophie said, holding in laughter.

"Knock it off," I said, dejected.

Apparently, my lips stretched all the way to my ears.

Finally, Maddie looked at Sophie and said, "Aww done," handing the lipstick to Sophie.

But the damage had been done. To my face, my ego, and most likely, Sophie's opinion of me.

Before I could regroup, Maddie yelled, "I want gasses!"

"I think she wants me to fart," I said, chuckling.

"No, dummy. She wants your glasses."

"Oh, glad we discussed that first," I said, chuckling. "No, sorry Maddie. You can't have these."

"Want gasses!"

"How about I fart instead?" I asked.

Sophie smirked at me and rolled her eyes.

Maddie yelled, "Want gasses!" She then ripped the glasses off my face and snapped them at the bridge.

"Ahhh, farts," I said, annoyed.

"Oopth," Maddie said.

Sophie's eyes bulged, as she looked at my two monocles. "Do you know the Oculus Reparo incantation?"

"Sadly, no. While I may look like Harry Potter, with more stylish hair, I have no magical ability."

"Well, before Harry knew he was a wizard, he just used tape, right?"

"Yep," I said, trying not to be annoyed. I was happy that she knew her Harry Potter, but still not enthused about my glasses. But I had little time to stew.

Maddie interjected, "Pee pee!"

"Do you have to go pee pee?" Sophie asked.

"No, pee pee. Aww done!"

"You made pee pee already?" I asked.

"She's not potty trained yet. I need the diapers. I'll change her."

Thank God. I wanted nothing to do with the diaper scene. "Where are they?" I asked.

"They're over there," Sophie said, holding Maddie out in front of her, arms locked at the elbows.

"Over where?"

"There!" Sophie said, turning and nodding toward the couch with her head, which was completely empty. Her head wasn't empty. The couch was. "I thought they were there. Ummm, can you check in the kitchen? It's a pink diaper bag."

I ran into the kitchen, as Maddie kicked and screamed. "Pee pee! Wet!"

I scoured high and low, no pink diaper bag anywhere to be found. I checked under chairs, in cabinets, and even a few drawers where the bag had no chance of fitting. It was a mystery. It reminded me of The Comic Con when my favorite author, C.T. Walsh, had problems with his man bag. Only this time, Thor's hammer didn't go up my butt. And for that, I was thankful.

"Hurry up! She's soaking wet!" Sophie yelled, panicked.

"It's not here!" I scanned the kitchen for something that could help. And then I saw a roll of paper towels. I grabbed the roll, tucked it under my arm like a football, and took off running back to the den.

"Oh, no! I think they left it in the trunk of the car when we went shopping!" Sophie yelled from the den.

I spun around a corner, narrowly missed tripping on a statue, and promptly tripped over Baxter, Sophie's dog. We both yelped, as I hurdled forward into the den, and crash landed onto the floor with a thud and an "Ahhhh, farts!" Which, apparently, Maddie found very amusing. At least I held onto the paper towels. Mr. Muscalini, my gym teacher, would've been proud. My body throbbed, but it would've been worse if I didn't grab the extra-absorbent paper towel roll that muted my fall.

"Are you okay?" Sophie asked, more amused than concerned.

"Spectacular," I groaned, handing her the paper towels.

"What the heck am I gonna do with this?" Sophie asked.

"Wrap it around her like a diaper. We can tape it on," I said, making it up as I went along.

"We have duct tape in the garage, but are you sure you want to go there?"

"Into the garage?"

"To the duct tape," Sophie said, laughing.

"Very funny," I said, heading to the garage.

"Duck. Quack. Quack," Maddie said.

I headed out and made my way to the garage. I quickly

found the duct tape and returned to the den. Sophie had already wrapped Maddie with the entire paper towel roll.

"She looks like a mummy," Sophie said, dissatisfied. "It's up to her chest."

"No, that's good! We need maximum absorption," I said, picking at the edge of the duct tape.

"Mommy?" Maddie asked, curiously. "Where Mommy?"

"Oh, no, sweetie. She's not here yet," Sophie said, her eyes bulging.

"I want Mommy!" Maddie yelled.

"Quick! The diaper's not gonna hold!" Sophie yelled.

I tore off a piece of duct tape and attempted to secure the makeshift diaper while Sophie struggled to keep Maddie still. Tears streamed down Maddie's face, as she continued to whine about her mommy.

Just as I was about to tape one side of the diaper, Baxter surged into the room, excited for all the 'fun' and promptly chomped onto the end of the duct tape and pulled at it like it was a chew toy.

"Baxter, no!" Sophie yelled.

Baxter apparently had hearing issues, because he continued tugging on the duct tape. Instead of fighting with him over the tape, I let it go and tore off another one. I reached to put it on Maddie, who was still crying and wiggling from Sophie's grip, and actually connected with the target, securing the left side of the diaper.

I tore off another piece of tape and dove for Maddie while she broke out of Sophie's hold. I missed the diaper, but connected with Sophie's face, planting the tape right across her eyes.

"Austin!"

I was distracted by Baxter's coughing. I left Sophie in a blinded state to see Baxter retching on the floor. I looked around and couldn't find the piece of duct tape that Baxter had stolen from me.

"I think he ate the tape!" I yelled.

Sophie tore the tape off her face with a yelp. When we turned to find Baxter and Maddie, the good news was that they were together. The bad news was that Maddie was on Baxter's back with both hands wrapped around his tail, and pulling up, seemingly farther then physics should've allowed. Baxter took off running. Maddie bounced from side to side, as they disappeared into the hallway.

"Baxter!" Sophie yelled, giving chase.

I was right behind her. We made our way into the kitchen to find Baxter sprinting in a circle, still attempting to hack up the duct tape, dragging Maggie across the tile floor on her back, seemingly having the time of her life. Baxter was not as enthused.

"Maddie, no!" Sophie yelled. "You're hurting Baxter."

Maddie let go of Baxter, who disappeared under the kitchen table. Maddie started to cry. Again. "Hurt Baxter?"

"It's okay, sweetie," Sophie said, picking her up.

"Are you hungry?" I asked, attempting to change the subject. I had remembered Maddie's mom saying something about food.

"Hungry!"

"Nice call," Sophie said, plopping Maddie into a high chair next to the table.

"I'll heat up the pasta," I said, hoping I wouldn't have to entertain Maddie. I had lipstick all over my face. I didn't know what would be next. Eye shadow? A new hairstyle? I was good on both. For the record, I was not already wearing eye shadow. I didn't have any and didn't need any.

"Thanks," Sophie said, barely paying attention to me. She was busy playing Boop on Maddie's nose.

I found the pasta in the fridge and threw it into the microwave. It was good to go forty seconds later. I grabbed the bowl, tested the temperature, and handed it to Sophie.

"I'll feed this to her if you order the pizza," Sophie said.

"Done," I said, grabbing my phone. But it was not done.

Maddie grabbed a handful of spaghetti and sauce and threw it at Sophie, connecting with her shirt.

"Maddie, no!"

Maddie then grabbed the bowl out of Sophie's hand and dumped it over her own head. She put the bowl down and proceeded to pick up the random pieces of spaghetti and munched on them as if it was a socially-accepted method of eating.

Sophie and I just stared at each other, mouths agape.

I was jolted back when Baxter heaved and then hurled a slimy piece of duct tape onto the floor and then licked up some spaghetti beneath Maddie's tray.

"Umm, now what?" I asked.

"We just let her be."

Sophie cleaned up Maddie's hair while Maddie happily ate, feeding Baxter from time to time. When she was done, Sophie cleaned out the dish and put it into the sink while I cleaned up the floor.

When I was done, I looked up to see Maddie hunched over, snoring.

I nodded to Sophie, careful not to say anything to wake the baby.

"Thank God," she mouthed. "Let's get her to bed."

We slowly and quietly unhooked the tray from the high chair and removed Maddie. Her mummy diaper looked a tad damp, but I wasn't about to suggest we change it. Her parents were just going to have to deal with it.

Sophie carried Maddie up the stairs and down the hall. I

followed her into a bedroom, stuffed with suitcases, baby toys, and a pack 'n play crib. Sophie lay Maddie into the crib. She fussed and I almost needed my own roll of paper towels, but thankfully, Maddie didn't wake up.

We tiptoed across the room and into the hallway. Sophie closed the door. I exhaled, as we slinked away, our fingers crossed that Maddie would stay asleep, at least until her parents came home.

"I think that went well," Sophie said.

"I think I need a soothing coma," I countered.

Sophie led me back to the den. We both collapsed on the couch. I don't remember falling asleep, but I assure you that I remember waking up.

The words, "What the-" boomed into my ear.

I startled awake, not sure what was going on. I found myself nose to nose with Sophie's dad. It was only slightly uncomfortable. It was more than just the garlic mashed potatoes that he surely ate for dinner.

"Were you two kissing?" Sophie's dad yelled at me.

"Umm, no, sir," I said in a panic.

"Then why do you have lipstick on, Austin?" Sophie's dad asked, annoyed.He stood up and looked over at Sophie.

Sophie's Mom hurried over and said, "Take a deep breath." I was pretty sure she was talking to her husband, but I needed a few myself.

"Daddy, Maddie put it on him. It was the only thing that would get her to stop crying."

"Oh," he said, sheepishly. "Sorry."

I shrugged. It was the least of the issues we had faced that night.

Sophie's aunt and uncle walked into the den.

"What the heck happened here?" Sophie's uncle asked, staring at my face.

"And what happened with the diapers?" Sophie's aunt asked.

"We couldn't find the diaper bag. I think you left it in the car after shopping."

"So you used paper towels?" Sophie's aunt asked.

"That's what I would've done," Sophie's dad said.

"Yes," I said. "And to be honest, we're not overly thrilled with the absorption capabilities. You might want to give them a weak review on Amazon."

"Anything else I should be aware of?" Sophie's aunt asked.

"You didn't smash up the car or anything, did you, Austin?" Sophie's dad questioned.

I wasn't sure if he was kidding or not, but I took the joke route. I know, what else is new? "No, sir. She's in the garage good as new. She drives like a dream, though."

"Very funny."

"Ready for kids?" Sophie's mom asked me.

"No disrespect, but absolutely not."

Sophie's parents laughed.

I looked at Sophie's aunt and uncle, who were not as enthused and said, "She's a doll, though." A crazy, lunatic doll, but a doll, nonetheless. Little did I know that crazed, lunatic dolls would nearly destroy my life. But we'll get to that.

Anyway, Sophie and I decided it would be best if we never discussed our babysitting adventure ever again. And thankfully, the rest of the weekend wasn't anywhere nearly as 'exciting' as Maddie had been.

3
——————

I was on my way to school on Monday morning. I bounced on the high school bus next to Barnie "Barn Door" Herbert. You may recall that I only go to the high school for one period. I take science there and then head back to Cherry Avenue middle school to finish out my day. They had me skip eighth grade science and go straight to high school, which I was not happy about. First off, Sophie had been my lab partner, and now I had Flea, a cool enough dude, but not Sophie. We had our ups and downs, me and Flea. He blew my eye brows off a while back. They were still filling in almost two months later, but he did save me after I got duct taped to the school bus. Plus, Sophie was just a bit prettier than Flea.

It was Monday morning, so the bus shenanigans were at a minimum. Friday afternoons? Forget about it. I followed Barn Door out of the bus, unscathed. As I entered the school, I did a double take. There were kids standing in front of a duct tape art project on the wall.

"Thankfully, it wasn't us." I had been duct taped to the wall in high school more times than I care to admit.

"No, there's nobody stuck there," Barn Door said. "It's a shrine for Chase Griffin and Noah Braddick."

"Who are they?"

"I forget you're not here all day. They were expelled for the duct taping of Principal Buthaire."

"The kids who I caught? Got caught?" I corrected myself.

I had gotten tired of getting duct taped to every architectural structure in the school, so I set a trap for them, and ending up gluing them and our esteemed principal, who I named Prince Butt Hair, to the floor. Unfortunately, it cost him half his mustache. Butt Hair hadn't had much luck with his mustache over the past year or so. He lost both halves of his mustache to separate duct tape attacks. He was devastated. Frankly, his mustache was his best quality and the only thing I admired about him.

"There's a duct tape shrine for Chase and Noah? Why?"

"There's talk of someone starting it back up again. To fight the power."

"Oh, great. Just what we need."

"I thought it was pretty cool, actually. Not backing down to The Man."

"Yeah, but we're the ones always getting taped to things," I said.

Barney scratched his head. "Oh, right. That is a bad idea."

I STOOD with my crew in the Atrium, with the exception of Sophie and Cheryl Van Snoogle-Something. I tried to make it to this gathering every day, hustling from high school. I didn't always make it, but thankfully Prince Butt hair didn't give me detention that morning, so I was able to see Sophie and my friends. But all was not well.

"You want to grab pizza and watch an Avenger's movie this weekend?" Ben asked.

"It's Monday. Why are we talking about the weekend?" Sammie asked.

"Because it's Monday. Thinking about the weekend is the only thing that gets me through the week."

"I thought it was seeing me," Sammie said, slightly annoyed.

"It is, which is why I want to see you even more on the weekend."

Nice recovery, Benjamin. He usually got himself into more trouble than he got himself out of, which is what makes him so lovable.

"I don't even eat pizza, anymore," Sammie said.

"That's ridiculous," I said. I grabbed her by the shoulders and looked into her eyes. "Sammie, are you in there? Were you abducted by aliens?"

"Aren't we getting too old for pizza?" Sammie asked.

"That's...not possible," Ben said. His face morphed to worry. "Austin?"

Ben and Sammie were my oldest friends, and they were dating. It was not a situation I wanted to get in the middle of, but I had to defend my favorite food. Oh, and my best friend. "I don't think you grow out of pizza."

Sammie shrugged. "You definitely can grow out of superhero movies."

"Again, unlikely, but I will agree to disagree."

"You don't think they're a little immature? Why don't we watch a documentary?" Sammie asked.

"A what?" Luke asked. "I don't even know what that is."

"It's time you boys grew up," Cheryl said. "You need a little responsibility."

Unfortunately, responsibility was coming. Like an asteroid. And it was Judgement Day.

4

After school, we stood in the Atrium before boarding the buses home.

I heard a loud squeaking sound and immediately worried that someone had released a hoard of rats into the school. Not that I had ever been a part of something like that, unless, of course, you heard me tell that particular story. The sound was not rats. It was, in fact, four ginormous carts filled to the brim with packaged boxes.

"What's going on here?" Ben asked.

"It's probably plutonium for the radioactive beef stew," I said, shrugging. We were used to it at that point.

"Wouldn't they be in a hazmat suit?" Ben said.

Sophie squinted her eyes, reading the boxes, and asked, "What's a Baby Bot?"

I felt all the blood rush from my face. "Oh, no...It's... happening," I said, softly. "Our lives will never be the same. Tell your parents you love them. We might not all make it through this. Let's run away together," I pleaded with Sophie.

"Stop being so dramatic," Sophie said, smirking.

I grabbed her by the shoulders, ignoring her comment, and looked deep into her beautiful eyes. "Let me look at you one last time before your innocence is gone. Before that wonder in your eyes is snuffed out by a soul-sucking robot."

"What are you talking about?" Sophie asked.

"Soul-sucking robots? That sounds like something Ben would watch," Sammie said, snottily.

"Sorry, Miss I'm-Too-Mature-To-Eat-Pizza," Ben said, annoyed.

"Baby Bots. They will crush you," I said, already weary from the experience.

There's only so much I can tell you about it. You pretty much have to see them in action, so let's just skip to the next day in Home Economics and Health class.

I sat in class with Sophie, Ben, Sammie, Just Charles, Cheryl, Luke, Randy, Regan, Ditzy Dayna, and Kami Rahm, among others. It was the first day of a new marking period. My crew sat across the room by the windows, as far away from Randy and Regan as possible.

I was still emotionally drained. "This is gonna be terrible. It's been nice knowing ya."

"Yeah," Ben added. "I don't think I'm gonna graduate and make it to high school."

Sammie said, "Even Flea made it through middle school."

"He's a football player. He got special treatment," I said. "We're not gonna make it. We'll be stuck in the mayhem of middle school forever."

"Why is this going to be so bad?" Sophie asked. "It's just health and home life. The human body, cooking, and stuff."

I looked at her and chuckled nervously. "It's more than cooking. It's the apocalypse. With homework."

Before I could explain, a woman walked into the class. "Good morning, class. My name is Mrs. Flaum."

"Phlegm?" Regan asked.

"Flaum."

"Phelgm?"

"Flaum."

"Flaum?" Regan asked.

Mrs. Flaum said, "Phlegm...err. Let's get started. "It's going to be an exciting few months for us here. Judging by the smiling faces, some of you know why."

She was wrong. The smiling faces were all from unsuspecting people like Sophie who had no idea what we were in for, while those of us who were miserable, knew full well what was coming.

Mrs. Flaum continued excitedly, "Well, instead of telling you about it, why don't I just show you?" She walked to the corner of the room. In my dazed and drained state, I hadn't even noticed the baby carriage behind her desk. Mrs. Flaum wheeled the carriage in front of everyone, leaned over, and pulled out a somewhat realistic-looking baby.

Ditzy Dayna asked, "You keep your baby in the back of the classroom all day? What a good baby. I had no idea it was even there."

Mrs. Flaum smiled. "It may look like a real baby, but it's not." She held it up over her head, like she was Rafiki in the Lion King, holding the new-born Simba in front of the herds of animals. "I give you the Baby Bot 2000!"

There were a few cheers and claps, and a few groans, as well.

"It cries like a real baby, coos like a real baby, AND has explosive diarrhea like a real baby. You're gonna love this."

"Sounds lovely," I whispered to Sophie.

"It's gonna be so easy. We took care of a real baby over the weekend."

"Yeah, and we almost died," I said.

Sophie chuckled. "You're always so dramatic. This can't be anywhere close to as hard as that."

Kami Rahm raised her hand and said, "My brother had the original Baby Bot two years ago. It was miserable."

Mrs. Flaum shook her head. "I know, but this is new and improved! Not to worry. The technological improvements that have been made since the last model are off the charts. Now, you will each have a partner and share responsibility for taking care of your assigned baby. The baby is smarter than most of you. It has a sophisticated computer system that will track and report on your caregiving abilities, whether you feed him, soothe her when she cries, or change his diapers promptly."

"We have to change diapers?" Randy asked, disgusted. "That's ridiculous."

"That's life as a parent," Mrs. Flaum said, simply.

"But we're in middle school," I added.

"Nobody said life was easy. When I was your age, I delivered all six of my siblings before I was nine years old."

"That's not really true," Luke said.

"You don't have to believe me about that, but you should believe me about this- babies are the future. And the future is now."

Huh?

OH. My. God. It was going to be terrible. Caring for the Baby Bot 2000 would be like babysitting Sophie's cousin, Maddie, only worse. It would actually tell our teacher how bad we were at caring for it! And it would be for weeks at a time, not just one dinner out. We were going to get crushed.

While Mrs. Flaum handed out the class curriculum, we all chatted about the goods and many bads of Baby Bots.

"This is really exciting," Sophie said, her eyes lighting up, as she stared at the Baby Bot 2000. "I want my parents to have another baby. Having Maddie around has been so much fun."

I wasn't sure if she hit her head or something when we babysat Maddie. It was chaos. I didn't know what to say. Or maybe she hadn't seen all of it because she had duct tape glue in her eyes.

Sophie continued, "My brother is getting too old and annoying."

"That's what brothers do," I said, my brother Derek popping into my mind. "What if you get another one?" The thought of two Dereks almost made me puke.

"I hadn't thought of that," she said, pursing her lips.

"Where are our babies now?" Ditzy Dayna asked.

Mrs. Flaum answered, "The stork will bring them to the Atrium after school."

"I knew babies came from storks!" Ditzy Dayna said. A bunch of kids chuckled.

"This is health class. Don't you think we should avoid perpetuating inaccurate reproductive information?" Cheryl asked.

"There will be time for that, dear. For now, that's how things are. Now, groups will be boy-girl. You can create them yourselves. Talk amongst yourselves and figure it out. The buses will be held after school. We will hand out the babies in the Atrium. You should get together with your partner later tonight or this weekend to discuss care taking and parenting philosophy. The baby's care will begin on Monday."

"Parenting philosophy?" Ben asked.

I shrugged. "You feed it, burp it, change its diaper, and put it to sleep. What kind of philosophy do we need?"

I was quite wrong. Not only would we need a parenting philosophy, the Baby Bot 2000 would make us question all levels of philosophy: why we're here on this Earth, the meaning of the universe, and how can little, tiny, baby robots puke and poop so much stuff?

∽

AFTER THE FINAL bell of the day rang, I met Sophie outside her classroom so we could head to the Atrium together to get our robot. There was a crowd surrounding Zorch and Mr. Muscalini when we arrived in the Atrium. They stood in front of giant bins of Baby Bots.

Sophie shook her head. "That's hardly good care for our babies."

"They're fake babies," I said.

Mr. Muscalini's voice boomed. "Okay, let's get started." He grabbed a baby from the bin, eyed Randy Warblemacher, my chief nemesis, and said, "Give me a ten yard square out."

"But sir, I'm the quarterback."

Mr. Muscalini raised an eyebrow.

"Yes, coach." Randy lined up while Mr. Muscalini held the baby like a football.

Mr. Muscalini squatted down and held the baby out in front of him with one hand. "Blue forty two, hut, hut, hike!"

Everyone watched Randy run through the crowd with ten steps and abruptly cut left, the Baby Bot 2000 spiraling out of Mr. Muscalini's hand.

Caught by surprise, I froze, as Randy's body surged toward me, his hands outstretched to catch the baby. The Baby Bot 2000 landed softly in Randy's hands. His momentum was not as soft. Randy barreled toward me, dropped his shoulder, and leveled me to the ground. My teeth chattered. My brain felt like it just got out of the spin cycle of a washing machine. I finally knew how Flat Stanley felt. I lay there moaning, waiting for someone to peel me off the floor. "Austin! Are you okay?" Sophie asked, kneeling on the ground next to me.

"Hey, Davenfart. Is that you down there?" Randy said with laughter. "Kind of reminded me of the time when you dropped baby Jesus in the Santukkah! play, only the opposite." Randy looked around at all the girls smiling at him like idiots. "Not bad for a quarterback, eh ladies?"

Everyone else was laughing at me. I had become immune to it, plus I was more concerned whether or not all my parts were still attached to my body.

Randy had brought up one of my darkest moments, but it wasn't one of Randy's brightest, either. I sat up.

Sophie stood up in Randy's face. "You mean when you were puking your guts out in the manger?"

Randy handed the Baby Bot 2000 to his smirking girlfriend, Regan, and walked away, chuckling.

Ben and Luke hurried over and helped me off the floor.

"You good?" Ben asked.

"Spectacular," I said. "Can we run that play again?"

Little did I know, getting run over by Randy would be one of the highlights of my Baby Bot experience. Yep. It was that bad.

Mrs. Flaum cut through the crowd, fury in her eyes. She headed toward Zorch and Mr. Muscalini. Zorch seemingly sensed what was coming and started polishing the already-sparkling trophy case behind him.

"Mr. Muscalini! That is hardly the example I want set for these children. They are supposed to learn to care for those babies like they were real infants. How are they to respect this process if you toss them around like toys?"

"A football is not a toy," Mr. Muscalini countered.

"You're missing the point. Maybe if you spent some time working out your brain and not your ridiculously oversized arms, you might act like a civilized human being," Mrs. Flaum said, pointedly.

Mr. Muscalini again missed the point. He flexed his

bicep. "Thank you for the compliment, but that's not really my thing."

Mrs. Flaum shook her head. "Mr. Zorch? Perhaps you could help me?"

"Oh, of course," Zorch said. "I didn't realize you were there."

My ears finally stopped ringing and I was no longer seeing two of everything. Imagine how big Mr. Muscalini's arms looked like with double vision. It was ridiculous.

"Okay," Mrs. Flaum said, staring at the clipboard in her hand. "When I call your name, please step forward to take your baby from Mr. Zorch."

It was time. Sophie and I stood beside Ben and Sammie.

"I hope we get a good baby," Sophie said.

"I hope mine's cute," Sammie said.

"I just want mine to keep his mouth shut," Ben said.

Sophie and Sammie both shot him a look. I had a lot I wanted to say, but after that, I just bit my tongue.

"Benjamin Gordon and Samantha Howell," Mrs. Flaum called out.

"I've waited for this my whole life," Sammie said, rushing forward.

Zorch held the Baby Bot 2000 out for her and said to Mrs. Flaum, "They get baby number eight."

Mrs. Flaum wrote down something on her clipboard, as Sammie hurried back to us, nearly in tears. She squeezed the Baby Bot 2000 in her arms and asked, "Isn't he beautiful?"

"So cute," Sophie gushed.

Ben and I looked at each other. I shrugged and said, "It's a doll. It's not a real baby."

Sammie shook her head. "You just don't get it."

"Before you get mad at me, talk to my sister. She nearly

pulled all her hair out in eighth grade and almost became a nun."

Sophie rolled her eyes and Sammie.

Mrs. Flaum called out, "Sophia Rodriguez and Austin Davenport."

"It's Davenfart!" Randy yelled out to laughter.

Mrs. Flaum looked at me. "Do I have a typo? Is your name really Davenfart?"

"No. He's just an idiot," I said.

Zorch held the baby out for Sophie and said, "Congratulations. It's a boy."

"Thank you!" Sophie said, leaving me in a cloud of dust. No disrespect to Zorch.

I smiled at Zorch and headed back to my crew. Sammie and Sophie were admiring the Baby Bots, smiling from ear to ear.

Luke got called up with Ditzy Dayna. That was gonna be an interesting parenting pair.

Sophie looked at me. "Don't you want to see our baby?"

"Of course," I said. I peeked over Sophie's shoulder, as she held the Baby Bot 2000 in her arms. My eyes nearly bulged out of my head. "Aaaahhhh, farts!"

"What's wrong?" Sophie asked in a high-pitched panic.

I pointed to the Baby Bot's face. "It has a giant butt chin. Unbelievable."

"It's cute," Sophie said. "I like it."

"It's the bane of my existence," I said. The stupid robot baby looked like my brother, Derek. "Can we get another one?"

Sophie jolted back and clutched her heart. "You want to trade our baby?" she scoffed.

Sammie looked at me, disgusted, and said, "Unbelievable."

Immediately, I knew I had made a horrible mistake, but I wasn't sure what to do. "I'll just deal with it," I said. That wasn't overly helpful, either.

Sophie looked at Sammie and said, "Oh, what a great parent. He'll just deal with it."

Mrs. Flaum called out, "Charles Zaino and Cheryl Van Snoogle-Something."

"Oh, baby Van Snoogle-Something has arrived!" Cheryl said, rushing to Zorch.

"Act like you care," I whispered to Just Charles.

Sophie looked at me, shocked. "Don't you want to hold our baby?"

I nodded. "Absolutely." Not.

I SAT with my family in a booth at Burger Boys. It was packed, which was surprising on Taco Tuesday. I sat crammed in between Derek and Leighton.

"Sorry about the booth, kids," my mother said.

"Why couldn't we just sit by the kitchen? There was a big table open over there." Derek asked, annoyed.

"Don't worry about it," my mother said.

"Mom, we're all teenagers. That's not an appropriate answer," Leighton said, annoyed.

"Austin's not a teenager yet. He's still a baby-waby," Derek added like a doofus.

My mother looked up like she didn't hear my sister's question. "Hmmm? Oh, the smells are a little too strong over there," she answered.

"Who can get enough of that bacon smell?" my dad countered.

Mom shot Dad a look and then grabbed her menu. She

studied it and said to no one in particular, "I...am...craving...a...burger."

"I want to eat cheeseburgers every day," I said.

And then out of the corner of my eye, I saw something that made me lose my appetite, which was tough to do at Burger Boys. Across the restaurant sat one Randy Warblemacher. He was sitting next to Regan and across from an unfamiliar man. I knew what both of their fathers looked like and that guy was not either of them. I held my menu up to my face and peeked around it. I know, I'm destined for the FBI or an international spy or something.

"What are you doing, dork?" Derek asked.

"Covert ops. You wouldn't understand," I said, simply.

I ignored the rest of his mutterings about me being an even bigger dork, my eyes locked on Randy and his dinner guest. I wish I had my phone out, so I could've snapped a pic of what I saw next. The man pushed an oversized, yellow envelope across the table toward Randy, who picked it up with a smirk. He flipped open the flap of the envelope and peered into it. He smiled, handed the envelope to Regan, and then slid his own, smaller envelope across the table to the man, who joined Randy in smiles.

"What is he up to?" I asked out loud. Whatever it was. It was nefarious. Nefarious, I tell you.

Derek nudged my elbow. "Will you hurry up already? The waitress isn't coming over because you're doing your stupid covert ops."

"Oh, sorry," I said. I looked at my mom and asked, "Can you get me a Bacon Boy with cheese? Medium?"

My mother nodded.

I slid out of the booth past Leighton. I had to get a closer look at who the dude was. I slipped around the bus boy station and took cover by a giant plant next to the bathroom entrance. I peered through some palm leaves, camouflaged better than a ghost.

"What are you doing?" A waitress asked me, annoyed.

Apparently, she had superpowers. Taken aback that she had made me so easily, I stammered. "I...ummm...well, just going to the bathroom."

"In the plant?"

I laughed nervously. "No. Long story. See you later," I said, with an awkward wave and scooted around the plant, into the bathroom.

As I entered, I hoped to see Max Mulvihill, my friend and bathroom attendant from school. He was always popping up somewhere. I didn't know where he went at night, so working the bathroom at Burger Boys was as good a guess as anywhere. Unfortunately, he wasn't there. But, someone else joined me shortly after I entered. I glanced over my shoulder as I did my business. It was Randy!

Normally, I wasn't enthused to see my nemesis. He always had some sort of biting comment or flat-out ran me over, but after witnessing what appeared to be nefarious dealings, I was intrigued. "What are you doing here, Randy?"

"A, umm, date," he said, quickly, and looked away.

Hmm, he didn't call me Davenfart or try to insult me in any way. Things were getting interesting. "Oh, Regan's here? Was that her father there in the suit?"

"Umm, yeah. He took us to dinner. He works a lot. Wanted to spend some time with Regan."

"Oh, isn't that nice. Does she have two dads?"

"No. What are you talking about?"

"Well, I've seen her father at school and that wasn't him."

"You're wrong, as usual, Davenfart." Randy washed his hands and exited without even drying them. Something was going on, but I didn't know what or how to figure it out.

I washed and dried my hands, and then hurried out of the bathroom to see if I could learn more about the mystery man. The three of them were twenty feet away from me, heading out the door. I hurried over to the exit, nearly fell down the stairs, and wobbled into the parking lot. Randy was pulling Regan by the hand toward a crowded Main Street, while the suited fellow was already in his car, backing out of his parking space. I grabbed my phone and jotted down his license plate. I tried to take a picture of him, but I never got a clear shot of his face.

I didn't know what Randy was up to, but I was gonna find out.

5

My crew came over to my house that Friday night. Of course, we were having pizza in my basement, scattered around on couches, futons, and bean bag chairs. Sammie brought her own salad. I almost told Frank when I called in my order, but he would've been heartbroken.

Cheryl shuffled through a stack of papers. "Oh, man. This is gonna be a lot more difficult than just taking care of a baby. Have you read all this?"

Luke peeked over at the paperwork from his bean bag chair, nearly rolling off onto the floor. "What the heck is budgeting?"

Sophie rolled her eyes. "I took a look at it after school. We're gonna have to learn a whole bunch of home tasks-cooking, laundry, buying groceries, budgeting, and, of course, infant care."

"How is she going to grade us on the Baby Bot?" Ben asked.

"Don't you pay attention?" Cheryl asked. "It's a complex computer that will score how well we care for it."

"I'm just gonna feed mine pizza," Luke said. "Who doesn't love Frank's?"

"There are cooking lessons from Frank in the curriculum!" I yelled.

"Noyce," Ben said.

"And Miss Geller..." I said, disappointed.

"Oh, no," Sophie said.

Miss Geller was the head of the cafeteria staff. I was pretty certain we had the worst food in the state.

Ben added, "I am not curious about her curious chicken nor do I want to know what's in the seafood surprise. But I'm sure we would be very surprised."

I chimed in, "I'm not sure she even knows. Do you think she's trying to kill us, by the way?"

"She's so nice," Sammie said.

"I think it's a solid fifty-fifty," Ben said, in answer to my question.

"This is gonna be the hardest class in all of middle school," Luke said.

"It's the school of life, man," I said.

"We'll be fine," Sophie said.

We were not fine, but we'll get to that.

I LOVE HANGING out with my friends, but sometimes I just like to chill with just Sophie. It doesn't matter whether it's watching a movie, looking up at the stars, or raising our strange robotic school assignment, we always have fun. Well, most of the time.

It was the first night we would be graded on the care of Baby Bot 2000. We decided to spend as much time as possible together, so that we could learn and help each other, which was fine with me. It was going well enough. We had just finished dinner and were lounging on the couch in my den, just the two of us. Well, the two of us and the robot kid, who was asleep in my arms. I didn't want to move for fear of waking Baby Bot up.

Sophie looked at me and whispered, "I like spending this time with you."

"Me, too," I smiled. "There's nothing I'd rather do than hang out with you."

"Aww, you're so sweet."

The Baby Bot started to stir. I wasn't sure if it was our voices or just time to wake up. Its eyes fluttered and then stared at me for a minute, before exploding into tears. The crying was so extreme, I felt like I was getting blasted with a fog horn. And when you live with Derek Davenport, you know what it's like to get blasted with a fog horn.

I was so startled, I yelled, "Ahhh, farts!" and tossed the Baby Bot into the air.

Thankfully, I don't work out, so the collection of pinball machine parts that they constructed into a robot baby didn't go far. Sophie reached out her arms and captured the Baby Bot, which was still crying. I guess the ongoing tears are not that surprising, given that it had just gotten thrown into the air.

Sophie's eyes widened and then narrowed, as she stared me down. "You can't just throw our baby!"

I shrugged. "Sorry? It was an accident."

Sophie didn't have time to stay mad. The Baby Bot continued to wail. She stood up and paced around the room, shushing it. She looked at me, frantic. "He won't stop."

"Sing to it," I said.

"It?"

"Him," I corrected.

Sophie cleared her throat and started to sing, "Rockabye baby, on the tree top. When the wind blows, the cradle will rock." She looked at me and said, "He doesn't like it. What kind of mother am I that I can't get my baby to calm down by singing to him?"

I didn't want to go there. This was getting a little too crazy. It was a fake baby. But I wanted to help. "Maybe he likes rap music," I said, shrugging.

"Why would you think our baby likes rap music?"

"I like rap music."

The baby kept crying. Sophie took a deep breath. "All right. Just try it."

I stood up and leaned over the Baby Bot. "What up, what up, baby. Why you cryin' and actin' all shady?"

Sophie interrupted. "Our baby isn't acting shady. Babies cry."

"Sorry. Let me try a new rhyme." I thought for a moment. "You don't need to trip, little baby. All you gotta do is zip your lip, and don't act crazy."

Sophie rolled her eyes and turned her back on me. She tried to shush the baby as she walked around.

After a few minutes, the Baby Bot calmed down.

I said, "Perfect. Now, we can go back to quiet time together."

Sophie walked back toward me, en route to the Baby Bot's carrying case. I'm not sure if that's what they really call it, but that's what it looked like to me.

Baby Bot had a different idea. It vibrated in Sophie's arms and then let out a, "Huwullah!" that nearly shook the room.

I had never been in a monsoon before, but I imagine the experience is similar, except that I got doused with what seemed like an industrial-sized vat of baby puke.

"Oh. My. God," Sophie said, half laughing.

"I'm glad you find this funny," I said, wiping green goop from my face. "Where did this all come from? It's just a tiny little thing. And how do you not have anything on you? Did you point it at me or something?"

"I guess I just got lucky," Sophie said, smiling.

She didn't get that lucky. Baby Bot unleashed another demonic blast of baby puke out of its mouth like it was a fire hose. Sophie's head jerked back, the force of the puke nearly reaching Mach one. When the volcanic eruption ceased, it left Sophie dripping with green goop, too.

"I guess I deserved that," she said, holding the Baby Bot with one hand while wiping her face with the other. "What now?"

"Mom?" I yelled to the kitchen. "We need a little help."

My mother and Leighton hurried in. And then busted out, laughing.

"I'm glad you find this amusing," I said, less than amused.

"We don't," my mother said, through massive amounts of laughter.

"Can you help us?" I asked.

"I'm not touching that thing," Leighton said.

"I'll take Baby Bot only until you guys clean up," my mother said, still smiling.

"Okay. Great. I'll see you in about a week. Sophie and I need a power washing," I said, walking past them with Sophie and out of the room, hating the inventor of the Baby Bot with every fiber of my being.

Sophie and I regrouped back in the den. The Babybeast was fast asleep in its carrier. I half wondered if we should put the thing in a cage, but didn't know how to bring that up to Sophie. I guessed it wouldn't go over so well.

"My parents are going to be here soon," Sophie said. "What are we doing with our baby?"

"We have to figure out what nights we're going to take."

"Do you just want to do every other night?" Sophie asked.

"That's fair. That way, nobody gets creamed, or barfed on, two nights in a row, and over every two week period, we'll get the same number of school nights and weekend nights."

"Sounds like a lovely plan," Sophie said. "I'm kind of excited."

"How is that possible?"

She didn't answer me, but instead said, "I'll take the baby tonight and you take him tomorrow."

"Deal," I said. I loved robots, but the Baby Bot and I were not off to a good start and I needed a break. Yes, I realize it was the first day, but nerds are not known for their endurance.

6

I slept like, well, a baby. I met up with Sophie and the rest of the crew in the Atrium before middle school started. There were Baby Bots everywhere throughout the Atrium, nearly all of them fussing or crying. It sounded like the middle school chorus. As bad as the Baby Bot crying was, they may have actually been better than our chorus.

And it appeared as if half the eighth-grade class did not sleep as well as I did. It wasn't as bad as when my nemesis, Principal Buthaire/Butt Hair, banned all hair gel in the school, and we were reduced to Walking Dead zombies. Apparently, hair gel is more important than sleep.

I could tell Sophie was hurting, but she powered through it, like she always does.

"How was it?" I asked, concerned. "Baby Bot didn't set the house on fire with a crazy fart or anything, did it?"

She was too tired to get mad. "It was fine," she said. "Still working out some kinks."

"Good. I think it puked a year's worth of hurl yesterday after dinner. We should be good for a while."

"Mine hit the ceiling," Luke said. "I was kinda proud."

"When mine made a poop, it blasted right through the diaper!" Ben said. "Sprayed my mom right in the face."

"Ewww. That's so gross," Cheryl said. "How was your night, Charles?"

Just Charles shrugged. "Piece of cake. My mother took care of it most of the night."

"You're not supposed to do that," Cheryl said, annoyed.

"I don't really care," Just Charles said. "I don't want to get blasted in the face with puke or poo, thank you very much."

The bell rang, making more babies cry. Cheryl took the baby from Just Charles without a word, and headed off to Advisory.

"Looks like you're in trouble, dude," Ben said.

"It doesn't look like it. You are," I corrected.

Sophie took the Baby Bot and we said our goodbyes.

Just Charles and I headed down the hallway to our Advisory classroom.

"What the heck is going on around here, man? These Baby Bots are a nightmare," Just Charles said, shaking his head.

"You should've seen how much mine hurled on me and Sophie. This is my worst nightmare."

"Even worse than getting eaten by an alligator?"

"Umm, yep." It wasn't even close. Maybe I would change my mind if I was staring down a gator, but at that moment, the Baby Bot was more than I could handle.

UNFORTUNATELY, it was my turn to Baby Bot sit that night. I was not enthused. Plus, we had two of them in the house, as Derek was stuck with his, too. I was surprised he hadn't sweet-talked his partner into taking it every night. Girls usually just look deep into his butt chin and become mesmerized, eager to do whatever Derek asks of them.

So, first the good news. I didn't get puked on. That's where the good news ends. The bad news is that my parents believed my brother and I needed to take responsibility on our own, and refused to help. And Leighton, only two years removed from her own Baby Bot experience, seemingly moved out of the house, perhaps the country.

The two Baby Bots in our house seemed to have some sort of wireless connection. When one was asleep, the other attempted to wake it up. And vice versa. So, what ended up happening was that the Baby Bots each slept half the night while Derek and I slept never. Like at all.

It was 6:15 A.M., time to get up. I could barely move my body. My head throbbed like it was a ticking time bomb. Kind of like my Baby Bot. It was only a matter of time before it exploded with tears, puke, or worse.

I was a little bit late to Cherry Avenue after first period at the high school. I just didn't have that normal pep in my step. I usually hustled to see my friends in the Atrium before Advisory started, so I didn't get a chance to meet up with them before health and home ec, which was riveting stuff.

Mrs. Flaum kicked it off with an exciting overview. "Today, we're going to do some laundry."

"This stinks," I muttered, a little louder than I would've liked.

"Like your dirty underwear, Davenfart," Randy said to chuckles.

"Your underwear doesn't get dirty, Randy? I guess it's hard for the thong to get dirty."

Randy made a gesture that I can't discuss.

Mrs. Flaum continued, "For homework, go to my e-board, choose one of the casserole recipes and make it for your family dinner. Please have your parents sign a copy of the recipe and bring it in as proof that you did your homework."

Yay! Laundry and casseroles! That's what I got to do on my night off.

BABY BOT 2000 WAS WINNING. As you know, I was up half the night, trying to keep the robot beast from crying, but didn't do a good job of it. At all. I zoned out as I walked down the hall toward my math class. The other students all blurred together. The chatter and laughter seemed distant. And then my numb brain saw something shiny. I was attracted to it like a moth to a flame. I looked over at it. It was golden. It was a ring. On Zorch's finger. I had never seen him wear any jewelry, not even a watch. The school bell schedule was seared into his brain or something, so he didn't need one. The only shiny stuff I'd ever seen him with was his oversized ring of keys. He had so many, I used to think he was a dungeon master.

"Austin? You okay, little buddy?" Zorch said, staring down at me.

"Is that a wedding ring?" I asked, surprised.

"It's a promise ring," he said, beaming.

"What does that mean? Isn't that for lame high school kids who are trying to be cool?" I asked, my filter apparently shut down from exhaustion.

"Oh, wow. That hurts, buddy."

"Sorry, I'm exhausted. My brain isn't working properly."

"We got engaged. Miss Geller wanted me to wear a ring, too." Miss Geller was the head of the should-be-condemned cafeteria at Cherry Avenue. Zorch continued, "I wanted make her happy."

"I can certainly understand that," I said, nodding. "It's very shiny." I was zoning out again. "That's great news...Got to get...somewhere." I gave Zorch a high five and walked off.

I was happy for him. Even though his future kids would probably hurl weekly from Miss Geller's cooking, they weren't my problem. I had enough of my own kid problems.

"Austin, wait...I wanted to ask you something."

I stopped and turned back around. Zorch's face zoomed in and out.

"How do you feel about being the ring bearer?"

"Isn't that a job for little kids?"

Zorch shrugged. "I guess technically, but we don't have much family and you're important to me."

"Thanks, Zorch. I would be happy to. Just as long as nobody has to know."

"That won't be a problem. We're only inviting half the kids in the school to the wedding," he said, smirking.

"Wonderful," I said. I forced a smile and gave him a thumbs up.

"Don't worry. It's gonna be simple. We're not getting crazy. We already rented a hall and we're making the food ourselves. She's gonna make my favorite meatloaf," Zorch said, smiling.

Ahhh, farts! I suddenly had an urge to talk protein bars with Mr. Muscalini for the first time in my life. I also wondered if I should call all the local hospitals or the Center for Disease Control and warn them about what was gonna happen. It was going to be a wedding with the potential for a hundred deaths by toxic meatloaf. Not the typical responsibilities of a ring bearer, but what can you do?

I bumped into Sophie just before class. I was delirious

from exhaustion at that point. I caressed her face. "Oooh, red. So pretty."

"What the heck is wrong with you?"

I didn't have a good answer. "You're so pretty. You want to smoochie smoochie?"

"Austin! What's the matter?"

"Does something have to be wrong with me to want to smoochie smoochie?" I asked, as we headed into class.

"No, but you're acting weird."

"I do every Tuesday." I was so tired, I didn't even know if it was actually Tuesday. And then I yelled out, "Tacos! It's Tuesday!" The whole class looked at me like I was weird, but I wasn't going to go through the whole Tuesday thing again.

I sat in the kitchen that night, staring at my undone homework. I didn't have the brain capacity to get all that much done. Derek walked in after practice, dropped his stuff on the floor, and plopped down next to me.

"Yo, let's make a casserole together," Derek said, like it was as exciting as going to a rock concert.

"That's the strangest thing you've ever said to me. But, we do have to make one for homework."

"I'll download the recipe. You get the stuff out and make it all. And then I'll eat most of it."

"Yeah, that sounds fair. I'll make my own casserole."

"Awww, come on, Austin."

"I will gladly do half the work if you do the other half, but I'm not some dumb girl at school willing to do your homework for you just because you flash your butt at her."

My dad walked into the kitchen and asked, "Dumb girls do your homework for you? And why are you flashing your butt at people?"

"I meant butt chin," I said, but maybe he did that, too.

"No, dad. He's not serious," Derek said, shooting me a look.

"About what? The butt or the homework," I asked.

Derek ignored me.

My father said, "I'm not angry. I was actually hoping it was true. I was looking for answers on why your grades stink."

"They don't stink."

"His butt does," I added.

"Your last report card was basically a giant, rotting turd."

I tried not to laugh. It wasn't often my brother got the business from my parents. You know, because of his family butt chin and all.

"It wasn't that bad. I was busy with football. I don't have time to be a nerd like Austin."

"How much time did you spend playing Playstation with Jayden over the weekend?"

Derek stammered. "Umm, let me think...A few."

"A few what? Hours? Days? Get your act together, Derek. High school is coming."

"It's not easy being in high school," I said.

Derek shook his head at me. "But dad, you said you didn't care about how I did in school."

"You only remember what you want to remember. I also said, "'as long as you do your best.'"

"Oh," Derek said. His voice trailed off into silence. "I don't think I heard that part."

"Good talk," my dad said. "I hear you're making dinner tonight?"

THE NEXT DAY, we had a Baby Bot outing at Frank's with the whole gang. I guess misery loves company. We all picked at our pizza, not really saying much. The Baby Bots were asleep, so none of us wanted to wake them, plus we were all really tired.

Of course, Ditzy Dayna failed to realize what we were trying to do and said, "My Baby Bot didn't stop crying all night, so we just put it outside."

"It's a baby!" Sophie said.

"Shhh. No, it's not," I said.

"Sorry," Sophie said, like she was not at all sorry.

Dayna said, "My mother says it's a plastic doll with the devil's soul. She keeps dousing it in holy water."

"You'll probably lose points for that," Ben said.

"I think she's beyond that. She nearly fed the baby to the coyotes!" Cheryl said.

Just Charles chimed in, "We don't have coyotes. And she's right. It's just a doll. I don't know why everyone is getting so crazy."

"It's not just a doll," Cheryl spat.

"We have bigger problems than this," I said. "We need to figure these...Baby Bots out."

"Well, there's got to be a manual, right?" Luke said.

"Did you *see* a manual?" Sophie asked. "Babies don't come with a manual."

"No, I saw one," Luke said, rummaging through his Baby Bot's carry case. He pulled out a folded-up piece of paper and held it up for everyone to see. "Awww, yeah. Here it is."

"Oh, my God. Open it up," Sammie said. "I need instructions."

Sophie grabbed it from Luke's hand and read the front cover, "Baby Bot 2000 instructional manual. Hmm." She opened it up and read, "Babies don't come with manuals. Good luck! You'll figure it out or fail!"

"Ugh," Cheryl said.

Ben asked, "What about online?"

"Nice thinking, Benjamin," I said. "I'm sure there's some sort of Baby Bot 2000 cheat code or something."

Sophie said, "These babies are not video games that have cheat codes. They're the future." She rolled her eyes at Cheryl and Sammie.

I grabbed my phone. "Still, we should probably Google it, just in case." I ran a search for the Baby Bot 2000. The results were pretty interesting. "Oh, look, your mother's right, Dayna. This review says that Baby Bot 2000 *is* the devil."

"Maybe we should call the customer service line? Or email them or something," Ben said.

"Maybe we can trick them into giving us all the answers," Luke said.

"Yeah, I'm sure we will be able to outsmart a bunch of psychos while getting zero sleep for the past week," I said, sarcastically.

Luke dialed a number and put his phone on speaker. We waited about ten minutes before anyone picked up, which either wasn't great customer service or they were having a lot of issues with Baby Bot 2000.

"Baby Bot headquarters. How may I direct your call?" a woman's voice asked.

Luke's eyes bulged. He stammered.

"Hello?" the woman asked.

"Hi, there!" I said, somehow conjuring cheer from my dead body. "We are having some difficulty with our

Baby Bot 2000s. I was hoping we could get some advice."

"Is your baby defective?"

"Umm, yeah."

Sophie elbowed me.

"What seems to be the problem?" the woman asked.

I shrugged. "It won't stop crying. And puking. And pooping."

The woman chuckled. "That's what the Baby Bot 2000 does."

Ben chimed in. "It just cries? All. Dang. Day?"

The woman said, "You haven't unlocked the code to quieting the baby down."

"See! I told you there was a code," I whispered to Sophie. "Do you mind sharing that code?"

"I'm sorry. That's not something we can help you with. Is there anything else you need assistance with?"

I looked around at the rest of my crew. Disappointment was rampant. "No, I don't think so," I said.

"Well, thank you for calling Baby-"

Luke hung up the phone. We were in it for the long haul. There were no fixes. No short cuts. It was gonna be rough.

SOPHIE and I waited for my mom to pick us up after our outing at Frank's. We sat on the curb in the parking lot.

"I think we should name our baby," Sophie said.

"Do we have to?" Had I been getting the proper amount of sleep, I probably would've avoided saying this next part. "I think you're going a little too far. It's just a doll. But if you want to, we can just call it Bot. 2000 might be cool."

Sophie's face registered pain and confusion. At first, I

thought she was going to pass out, but then I was scared she might explode. And then she did.

"That's the kind of father you are? If we get another Baby Bot, are we just going to start numbering them? This could be number one and then next one will be number two?"

My eyes widened and my chest started pounding. "Of course not. I mean, I'd feel bad for whichever one was named number two. For obvious reasons."

"That's the only reason? Because our second baby would be numbered after poop?"

"Well, it's a doll. I mean, maybe we could skip number two and go with something edgy like Tre or something, instead of three."

"Yeah, let's not."

"Okay. What do you want to name or number the doll?" I asked.

"We're not numbering the doll. We need to treat this like a baby. How about Austin Junior?"

"He doesn't even look like me. The butt chin."

"Will you get over the family butt chin, already? You act like your whole life is one giant prison sentence because your brother has a cute dimple on his chin."

"You think his chin dimple is cute?" I asked, my voice rising an octave. My life was unraveling.

"Well, I did, but now, it's just annoying."

"Wow. This changes everything."

"Don't be so dramatic, Austin. What if we name the baby, Trevor?"

"Like the frog in Harry Potter?" I asked, annoyed.

"Well, not after the frog, specifically."

"No. It will be a frog to me. How about Mo?"

"Mo?" Sophie asked, like there was no way in the world the Baby Bot would be named Mo.

"Yeah. Why do you say it like I just kicked your grand-mother in the gut?"

Sophie took a deep breath and ignored my question. "How about Donovan?"

I shrugged. "Could be kinda cool if I can call him Donny."

"No way."

"Why not?" I asked, annoyed. "It's a doll."

"Ugh. You just don't get it."

"Apparently, not." I needed to change the subject. "Who's taking Baby Bot tonight?" I asked.

"His name is not Baby Bot. It's my night, but my mom asked if you could take Trevor tonight."

"What? Trevor?"

"At the time, that was his name," she said, like I was the dumbest kid in town.

"You named him without me?" I scoffed. "This is unre-al!" I didn't know why it was so unreal, because I didn't want to name the devil robot, anyway. I shook my head, "My mom is sick. I don't know."

"What's wrong?' she asked.

"Stomach bug. She's puking everywhere. Kind of like Mo."

"Don't start," Sophie said.

I was actually hoping we were finished.

7

The next morning, I stood in gym class with Ben, waiting for Mr. Muscalini to arrive. My stupid Baby Bot was in the stroller in front of me. It was the boys' day to have the Baby Bots during school, so they were lined up down the entire baseline of the basketball court as we awaited our esteemed, oversized gym teacher. While I was fighting with Sophie about what our doll should be named, the 'cool' kids in gym class were all making up new nicknames for each other. As if Randy wasn't pretentious enough already.

Danny Freiss called out to Randy, as he exited the locker room. "Yo, R-Money! What's goin' on, dude?"

Randy called out. "D-Train!"

I looked up at the ceiling. "Oh, God. Middle School just got even more unbearable."

Randy called over to me, "Davenfart, you're looking even more disagreeable than usual."

I looked at him, frowning. "You're more unbearable than usual, R-Monkey."

"It's R-Money, Davenfart. Get it right or your baby gets it."

"It's a plastic baby, R-Monkey. Threaten it all you want."

The conversation ended as Mr. Muscalini stomped into the gym and turned to face us, his hands on his hips. His short shorts revealed his rippling quads and his Grimmwolf t-shirt was two sizes too small. I'm not sure if he grew into it or had never taken home economics himself, perhaps having shrunk it doing the laundry.

Mr. Muscalini looked at the rag-tag squad of students, half of us with Baby Bots in strollers, and said, "Take a look at my latissimus dorsi. Do I look like a cobra when I do this?" He flexed his back muscles, seemingly as hard as he could, the strain showing across his face.

He eased up and asked, "Well?"

Nobody said anything.

"Davenport, what do you think?"

"Umm, what's your latissimus dorsi?"

Mr. Muscalini shook his head. "Gordo?"

Ben pointed to me and said, "What he said."

Mr. Muscalini bellowed, "This is unacceptable! We're gonna run until you learn that my lats make me look like a cobra!"

"Nice work, Davenfart," Randy called out.

"But, sir?" I asked. "What about the Baby Bots?"

"Take them with you. I'm not going to be responsible for those mechanical mischief makers. Now, go! Go! Go!"

I grabbed the stroller and took off behind the crowd. I didn't know how this was going to teach us anything about Mr. Muscalini's latissimus dorsi. There were some things we learned about his ego and mental state, though.

We rushed outside and headed onto the track. By the time we made it halfway around, my lungs were seemingly rejecting air, because I couldn't get enough of it. I gasped, as I continued running, hoping that the universe would do me a solid and keep my Baby Bot from waking up, and if, by some chance, it woke up, that there would not be something solid or liquid in its diaper.

Consumed with air consumption and attempting to remain alive, I didn't notice my nemesis, Randy "R-Monkey" Warblemacher, approaching from behind me, seemingly having lapped me on my first lap of the day.

Before I knew what was happening, Randy surged forward on my right, his stroller speeding toward mine. My elite-level instincts kicked in. I swerved to avoid the incoming Baby Bot bomb. The wheel of my stroller caught the inside lip of the track and jerked hard to the left, darting onto the grass of the football field. I stumbled and fell to my knees, letting the stroller go with the hopes that it would roll to a stop.

Instead, Mo/Trevor/2000 slammed into the ground and skidded to a stop on the grass. I ran over to it, hoping it wouldn't cry. Hoping it wasn't dead. I wasn't sure the Baby Bots could die, but it would be just my luck if it was possible. Sophie might send me to meet the devil bot in the afterlife.

I picked up my Baby Bot and assessed the damage. It immediately burst into tears, nearly blasting my eardrums out of my head. Ben saddled up next to me. I wasn't sure how much he really wanted to help versus just not wanting to run.

"What's wrong?" Ben asked.

"What's wrong?" I asked, rudely. "This thing won't stop crying. And it has a goatee grass stain on its face!"

"Leave it. It's cool. Who doesn't want a goatee?"

"Umm, Sophie. Plus, my score just plummeted."

"Yeah, well, there's that. But he looks cool, so he'll be popular. Grades won't matter that much."

"But *my* grades do matter. And I don't have a goatee, butt chin, or the athletic prowess to get away with a failing grade.

I was terrified to find out what our score was. And of Sophie.

I DIDN'T HAVE any good answers for Sophie, other than to blame it on Randy and make sure Ben was there to help back me up. When I saw her for the first time with the Baby Bot, I didn't know what to say.

She looked down at the Baby Bot in the stroller. Her eyes nearly bulged out of her head. "What happened to our baby?" Sophie yelled.

I shrugged. "He wanted a soul patch?"

Ben added, "He's got your fashion sense."

"Seriously, what happened?" Sophie asked, concerned. She licked her finger and rubbed the Baby Bot goatee. It was still green as could be.

"Randy ran me off the track when we were taking the babies for a stroll. It wasn't my fault."

"You shouldn't have called him R-Monkey," Ben said.

"Not helping, Benjamin," I whispered.

Sophie huffed. "I don't need this aggravation. Can you take the baby tonight? I need to get some sleep."

"My mom is still sick."

"Well, I'm gonna be sick if I don't get some sleep," Sophie said, angrily. "Randy took the baby for an extra night. Regan says he's doing great."

I took a deep, calming breath. "Oh, that's a low blow. You've given me no choice. I'm not going to do anything because of Randy."

"Then do it for me," Sophie said, her hands on her hips.

I nodded. "That, I will do. Why don't you bring the baby over after school? We can practice making hamburgers together. We can have a nice dinner."

It was not a nice dinner. Well, unless endless plumes of smoke surging from your stove is your romantic version of a candlelit dinner. A very candlelit dinner.

I STOOD next to Sophie in front of the stove. The Baby Bot was fast asleep in the den. Our homework for the night was to practice making hamburgers. It sounded easy enough. I had seen my parents make a million hamburgers plus a countless number at Burger Boys. True, they were professionals, but how hard could it be? All you have to do is flip them. It turns out, they are more complicated than I thought.

We had eight carefully-hand-crafted beef patties sitting on a plate next to the stove, as Sophie ignited the stove and turned the heat to medium. "That should be good," she said.

"Let's chuck 'em in," I said, grabbing a burger and placing it into the pan. The burger sizzled as it touched the metal.

"Give them some space. You can probably fit four in there," Sophie said.

"Got it," I said, slipping the burgers into the pan. I looked down at the sizzling burgers and turned up the heat to high. Those babies were crackling and cooking like a champ.

Sophie looked at me and asked, "Are they sizzling too much? I think there's too much sizzle."

"You can't have too much sizzle when you're cooking meat. Every man knows this," I scoffed.

Sophie's eyes widened, as she took a step closer to me. "Only men know how to cook meat?" she asked. Quite confrontationally, I might add.

I took a step back, as the burgers continued their fabulous sizzle in the pan. "Umm, of course not. That would be ridiculous. But you obviously haven't been schooled on the subject of sizzle. Which is surprising, because you've been dating all this sizzle for two years." I raised an eyebrow and used my hands to display my sizzlingness.

And then, without warning, I began to cough uncontrollably. My vision went hazy. Sophie disappeared into a cloud of smoke.

"Must...find...oxygen..." I said, gasping.

Sophie was coughing, too. I pushed her to the side and sprinted to the back door of the kitchen. I jiggled the lock and tore the door open. Fresh, beautiful air surged into the kitchen.

The haze dissipated somewhat, so I could make out Sophie's shadow. I walked back toward her. "Are you okay?" I asked.

Sophie coughed. "Did you forget something?" She asked, annoyed.

"Not that I'm aware of," I said, knowing I was in a lot of trouble for something.

"You pushed me aside and left our baby in the burning house."

"The house wasn't burning, and I was opening the door so we could all breath. I saved your life! There should be a parade for me or something."

"Or something," Sophie said.

"Why did that happen?" I asked.

"We didn't put any spray or butter on the pan." She looked around and said, "It's still smoking in here. Why isn't it disappearing?" Sophie asked.

It's still burning!" I yelled. I rushed over to the stove and shut it off.

"Nice work, Mr. Sizzle. Your burgers could've burned down the house."

Before I could respond, the smoke detector started to beep.

"It's gonna wake the baby!" Sophie yelled.

I wasn't going to argue about whether or not it was a baby or a life-ruining doll.

"What if I hold his ears shut?" I asked, running into the den.

But it was too late. Baby Bot, Trevor, Mo, Soul-sucking creature, or whatever you want to call it had already burst out crying.

My mother rushed into the room, her face flush. "What's going on?' she asked, concerned. She pushed past me and hurried into the kitchen.

"Everything is fine. Just a minor snafu with some homework," I said, downplaying the incident.

I grabbed the baby and followed her into the kitchen. Sophie was using a dish towel to force the remaining smoke out of the open door.

"Is that raw meat?" my mother asked, looking at the uncooked burgers on the counter, and promptly hurled on Sophie's sneakers.

"Oh, my God. I'm so sorry," my mother said, standing up, as Sophie and I stared at her, in shock.

And then it got worse. I heard the roar of a fire engine off in the distance. I looked out the window to see Mrs.

Shikadance, our neighborhood cranky old lady, standing at the edge of the curb, staring at our house. It was not a good sign.

"Uh, we've got company," I said. "The fire department is here."

My mother took a deep breath, seemingly holding in more puke, and said, "I'll go talk to them."

"It's my fault. I'll do it and tell them everything is fine," I said.

"They're not gonna take your word that everything is a fine. You're a kid. No offense."

"Don't worry. I know these guys," I said, smirking at Sophie.

I handed Sophie the Baby Bot and slinked over to the front door and outside.

Officer Fontana from the First Responders' unit and Officer McGuire from the Fire Department exited their vehicles at the same time. They bumped shoulders as they both attempted to make it onto the walkway first. They jostled for the line leader position, with McGuire and his bulky frame eventually winning out.

"Hey, there he is!" McGuire yelled, giving me a thumbs up. "I didn't know you lived here. I tell everyone about how you got stuck in the doggie door and we got you out with butter. Everybody cracks up."

"I'm so happy they enjoy the story," I said.

"What's going on here? You burn down the house or something?"

Fontana cut in, "I'll be asking the questions. I'm the First Responder."

"Then why did I get here first?" McGuire asked, defiantly.

"Because you routinely don't follow protocol. You flout the rules. You're a flouterer."

It sounded like the conversations I had with my high school principal, Butt Hair.

My mother joined me outside, with Sophie not far behind. Thankfully, the Baby Bot had stopped crying.

McGuire huffed.

Fontana straightened his uniform and asked, "What's going on here?"

"We had a little mishap with some hamburgers on the stove. It's all taken care of."

"Well, I guess it's more dignifying than the time you got caught in the doggie door," Fontana said.

"It is," I said, annoyed.

"Grease fires are a serious risk," Fontana said. "They always seem to peak this time of year," he said, furrowing his brow.

"Yeah, I've noticed that," McGuire said.

"Yeah, because I just said it," Fontana argued.

"Gentlemen," my mother interrupted. "Will there be anything else?"

"We'll just take a quick peek and be on our way," McGuire said, sheepishly.

8

A fter we were finished talking to McGuire and Fontana, or should it be Fontana and McGuire? Never mind. Ben and Sammie showed up, pushing their Baby Bot in a stroller. We met them down at the street's edge.

"What happened?" Sammie asked, concerned.

"False alarm. Mrs. Shikadance sticking her nose where it doesn't belong," I said, angrily and loud enough for her to hear it. "Again." It was rude, but she was the neighbor that nobody wanted. Always calling the fire department when there's just a tad too much sizzle or the police when there's a car parked outside her house for too long. And don't get me started on her garden and lawn critiques.

"Mr. Sizzle here cooked the burgers on blast. Nearly killed our baby."

"Oh, no!" Sammie said.

"Mr. Sizzle? I like that," Ben said. "It's better than R-Money."

"I'm not sure you can kill a non-breathing device with smoke," I said, defensively.

Sophie shot a look at me.

"Well, since the house isn't burnt down, do you guys want to go for a walk? Our baby loves the outdoors," Sammie said.

"Aren't you taking this a tad too seriously? How could a robot like long walks through the neighborhood?" I asked.

I felt my body go cold, as Sammie glared at me. I looked at Sophie and she seemed to agree more with Sammie than me. I said, "Of course, we'd be happy to join."

About two minutes into the walk, our Baby Bot started to cry. I felt a pit in my stomach.

Sophie asked, "The baby's been with you all day. When was the last time he was fed?"

I shrugged. "Three hours ago, maybe?"

"You're not keeping a food diary?" Sophie asked, pointedly.

"What the heck is a food diary?" I asked.

Sammie chimed in, "You should be writing down what and when you feed the baby and then record its mood, bowel movements, etc."

"You want me to write down how often this thing poops?" I asked, shocked.

Sophie was even more shocked than I was. "This thing? This is our family."

"Do people give their families back after the semester is over?"

Based on Sophie's look, which rattled my soul, I decided to go along with her side. If she was right, it had phenomenal possibilities. I made a mental note to try to return Derek after the marking period was over.

"Okay. We'll try it," I said. I would do pretty much anything to get it to stop crying.

We circled back to the house to grab some food for the

Baby Bot. We stayed outside on my deck while we fed them. You know, because our robot kids liked to be one with nature.

We sat in Adirondack chairs around an unlit fire pit. I had Baby Bot on my lap with my feet propped up on the stone pit.

"It's food time, baby boy!" Ben said, excitedly.

I wasn't sure why Ben had jumped on the 'it's a real thing' bandwagon.

I shot a look at him and whispered, "What are you doing?"

"Just play along," he whispered back.

I shrugged looked at my Baby Bot. "It's time to burp, buddy boy."

Ben's Baby Bot let out a man-sized burp. Ben said, proudly, "My baby burps like a champ!"

"Yeah, that's gross," Sophie said.

Ben leaned in and baby-talked, "Can you burp the alphabet, little buddy?"

"My Bot won't burp. What's wrong with you, Baby Bot? Burp," I said.

I rhythmically patted my Baby Bot on the back, as Ben joined me in a chant of "Burp. Burp. Burp. Burp. Burp."

My Baby Bot burped like a frat boy. Ben and I cheered.

Sophie looked at Sammie, shaking her head. "It's no wonder boys grow up to be pigs."

I countered, "I think you need to pay closer attention in health class. That's not how it all works."

"Isn't it, though?" Sophie countered, annoyed.

I shrugged. "Anyway, you always said you wanted a pig."

"Yeah, a potbellied pig that doesn't grow up," Sophie said, smirking.

"That sounds like my dad," I said, laughing.

~

GYM CLASS WAS PRETTY interesting the next day. We stood on the baseline of the basketball court, waiting for Mr. Muscalini to emerge from his office. He surprised us by entering from the Atrium entrance, pushing a cart stacked with hockey pucks.

"Greetings, Gophers!" Mr. Muscalini bellowed. "I welcome you to what will likely be the best day of the year. It's the annual slapshot extravaganza!"

A few of the athletes, like Randy and Nick, cheered, but the rest of us were on the more cautious side.

"What does that entail, exactly?" Ian Kuster asked, most likely thinking what the rest of us nerds were thinking- were the athletes going to smash us with hockey pucks all period? Typically, if Mr. Muscalini was excited about something, it meant me and my nerd friends were about to get crushed.

The answer was, surprisingly, no. There would be no score kept and we weren't playing against anyone else, which meant Randy couldn't check me into the wall, slash me, and trip me with his hockey stick. I'm sure he was disappointed, but I didn't care. Finally, the nerds could enjoy gym class.

"So, line these puppies up, turn those hips, and let 'em rip!"

"What the heck are these things?" Randy asked, dropping one at his feet.

"They're hockey pucks, of course!" Mr. Muscalini said. "Fire when ready!"

Randy was right. For once. There was something odd about the hockey pucks. I shrugged, dropped a puck on the gym floor, and wound up. I unleashed a blast that soared across the gym and slammed into the wall. I didn't have a lot of experience actually connecting with a hockey puck, so I wasn't entirely sure what to expect, but my brother had once drilled me with hockey balls to prepare me for my medieval quest to become a knight (You may have heard that story before), and the sound the balls made bouncing off the garage door was significantly louder than the splat these particular pucks made. And I wasn't the only one who had suspicions.

"Sir, some of these are breaking apart?" someone called out.

"Yeah, I don't think I'm that strong," Ian Kuster said.

"And they don't look like hockey pucks," Randy added.

I pointed across the gym. "That one is sticking to the wall. What are these?"

Mr. Muscalini put his hands on his hips and stared at me. "I assure you, Davenport. They're hockey pucks. Made out of beef. Turned into hockey pucks by Ms. Hughes' class."

"Isn't that good protein?" Ben asked.

"Burnt protein is not good protein, Gordo! You ever hear of carcinogens?"

"Umm, yeah," Ben said, obviously not having any idea that carcinogens could potentially cause cancer.

I called out, "Isn't Zorch going to be mad about the mess? There's beef everywhere."

Mr. Muscalini furrowed his brow. "Why would Zorch be mad about my muscles? You think he's jealous?"

I shook my head and rolled my eyes. "No, I meant about the hamburger meat. All. Over. The. Gym."

"Oh, that. It's protein. I'm sure he'll be fine with it," Mr. Muscalini said, confidently.

Zorch wasn't fine with it. Not at all.

I RAN into Zorch later in the day. He was not his usual happy, engaged self. His shoulders slumped, as he walked slowly down the hallway.

"What's wrong? How's the wedding planning going?" I was hoping that maybe they no longer needed a middle school ring bearer.

"The wedding planning is going fine. It's Mr. Muscalini."

"What?" I asked, concerned. "Did he choke on a protein bar or something? Did he tear off your sleeves again, telling you that the sun's out so the guns should be out?" He did that to me once when he was helping us with our band. He thought showing my pencil-thin arms would somehow be rock-star like. It was not. Not at all.

"No," he said, without his usual chuckle. "He promised me he wouldn't do it again this year."

"What did he do?"

"He blew up a hamburger factory in the gymnasium. Or at least that's what it seems like."

"Oh, yeah. That. I think when you combine smashing stuff and protein in the same activity, it's very hard for Mr. Muscalini to resist."

"You're probably right. Next year, we'll have to prepare better. Take preventative measures."

I followed Zorch into the gym for moral support.

"Really, Mus? I thought we talked about this," Zorch said, annoyed. "I can't believe you would waste good protein like that."

"Those things were burned worse than your buns last year at the beach. That wasn't good protein."

"My buns or the burgers?" Zorch asked.

I covered my face with my hands. I couldn't listen to two oversized men talk about Zorch's burned buns.

And then I heard Mr. Muscalini's voice boom, "What's going on, Davenport? Why the long face?"

I didn't want to talk about Zorch's buns, so I told him my other woes. "I'm not getting any sleep and my stupid Baby Bot won't stop crying. Do you have kids? Maybe you could give me some tips."

Mr. Muscalini shook his head, pondering his words. It was something he didn't often do. "I'm offended."

My pulse tripled. "About what?" I asked.

"You're all my children."

"Oh, right. I meant, biological."

"Not unless Grimmwolf counts," Mr. Muscalini said. Grimmwolf was our stupid, savage mascot. A gopher with the heart of a lion and teeth of a great white shark. Mr. Muscalini continued, "But I can tell you about how I take care of Grimmwolf."

Ugh.

Mr. Muscalini continued, "I used to have to run with him in the stroller for hours until he fell asleep. It was good cardiovascular activity, too. It's always good to kill two birds with one stone. I wish I had been a cave man. I'd love to kill stuff with stones."

Zorch and I just looked at each other, not sure what to say.

Mr. Muscalini continued, "What?"

Zorch said, "He's a gopher. He needed you to put him to sleep?"

"He's my son. I wouldn't expect you to understand. Until you look deep into your child's eyes and see wonder looking back at you, you won't be able to grasp the power of love."

"I love pizza," I said.

"What? Pizza is not on the approved food list for bulking up," Mr. Muscalini boomed.

"I, umm, well," I said.

"Davenport, if you don't take your nutrition seriously, you're going to be a nerdy runt for the rest of your life."

I didn't know what to say. I just wanted to end it. "I'm glad we had this talk. It's been very helpful."

"We gotta fill out those sleeves so we can tear 'em off! Show those bowling-ball sized biceps off," Mr. Muscalini said.

I looked down at my bicep. "It seems like a long way from ping pong balls to bowling balls."

"Nobody said this was easy," Mr. Muscalini said, mesmerized by his own dancing pectoral muscles. "I love it when they do that."

IT WAS mayhem in my house. I don't know how parents do it. And I don't know how they expected middle school kids to do it. I had a crying Baby Bot in my arms, pacing around the kitchen, with dinner in the oven. Sophie was in the bathroom when the phone rang.

I picked it up and said, "Hello?" It was Barn Door. "Do I want to hang out? No...My whole life just exploded into parental pandemonium. I can't talk, man! I got a casserole in the oven, the dryer's going off, and the baby's screaming! Video games? Who has time for video games? I need a nanny...No, not for Baby Bot! For me!"

Sophie entered, frowning. She was probably angry that I wasn't giving our little bundle of joy my full attention. I also may have been yelling while the baby was crying.

"I gotta go, bro!" I said, hanging up before he could respond.

I shushed the Baby Bot, rocked it, and rapped to it. Nothing worked.

Sophie looked at me and said, "Give him to me. I'll do it."

"I can do it," I said, angrily.

"The baby can sense your mood," Sophie said. Irritably, I might add. "The baby knows you don't like him. So, he responds better to me."

"That's not true," I said.

Sophie reached over and put her hands on the baby. "Let go," she said.

I shook my head and let go of the ear-blasting Baby Bot.

As Sophie rocked the Baby Bot, I was conflicted. I wanted the soul-crushing screaming to end, but I didn't want her to think she was better than me. It took a little while for the Baby Bot to calm down, but not too long, so I guess it worked out okay. Sophie put the Baby Bot in the stroller in the den, and we headed to the basement to study.

As I collapsed onto a bean bag chair, I said, "Do you think that as eighth-grade President you can cancel the Baby Bot program?"

"I don't have control over student curriculum," Sophie said, simply.

"Why don't you take control of it?"

"That's not how it works."

"Why don't you make it how it works?" I asked.

"Ugh. There are defined roles, just like in real life. No government branch can just do whatever they want," Sophie said.

My dad creaked down the stairs to grab something. He

chimed in, "Have you seen some of the stuff the government does? It sure seems that way."

"Thanks, Dad."

"By the way, the baby just started crying. He's up in the den."

Sophie and I looked at each other, fear in our eyes.

I looked at my dad and smiled as hard as I could. "You want to spend some quality time with your grandson, pop?"

My dad laughed. "No can do. This is your project. I'm under strict orders not to help you."

I turned to Sophie. "Can you take him?"

"I was gonna ask you."

"Rock, paper, scissor?"

"I'm glad you're handling it the mature way," my dad said.

"Okay, I'll do it," I said, forcing my wiry and weary legs to stand.

I zombied my way up the stairs, down the hall, and into the den. I picked up the rude robot and held it close to my chest.

"It's okay, rude robot," I said, sweetly.

The Baby Bot cried the entire way back downstairs. When I got to the basement, Sophie was nearly asleep. She perked up when she heard the Baby Bot crying. I plopped onto the couch next to her. She grabbed a pacifier from her pocketbook and said, "Here's the pacifier."

She popped it right into my mouth. I almost fell asleep, instantly.

I said, "Blrble fribblenourse."

"What? Why are you talking like that?"

"Ruh?" And then I realized I had a pacifier in my mouth. I plucked it out. "This could be it."

"Sorry," she said, sheepishly. "I'm running on fumes."

The Baby Bot was finally quiet.

I whispered, "No, that's fine. I liked it. Do you have a bottle? I'm kinda thirsty. Regular milk is fine, but I prefer chocolate milk. I mean, I'd take Yoohoo if you got it."

Sophie shot me a dirty look.

"Okay. Maybe not."

Sophie got the baby to stop crying and put him to sleep in the carrier. She whispered, "By the way, I'm going out with my girlfriends Friday night. You'll have to take the baby."

"Okay. Maybe I'll have all the guys over with the babies. We can be miserable together."

Another dirty look.

"You're miserable now with me?"

"No. Just with the Baby Bot." The clarification didn't really seem to help.

9

It was girls' night out. Ahhhh, farts is right. That meant it was gonna be me and a whole bunch of Baby Bots. I invited all the boys to come over to my house with their Barf Bots, so we could all suffer together and offer emotional support, when needed. And it was gonna be needed often.

We chilled in the basement, as usual. We lounged around on the couch and bean bag chairs, in a moment of peace. All the Baby Bots were asleep.

"What are we doing tonight?" Ben asked.

I said, simply, "Movies, video games, pizza, and diapers."

"Diapers," Luke said, exasperated. "For robot dolls. This is ridiculous."

Just Charles wiped his brow. "Cheryl is driving me crazy. I think she likes the doll more than me."

"I think we all do," Ben said.

"Funny."

A fart reverberated from Luke's vicinity.

"Really, dude?" Just Charles asked.

"It wasn't me, man," Luke said. "It was the baby."

I turned up my nose. "That was a man fart," I said.

"Well, thanks for the compliment," Luke said, smiling. "My Baby Bot farts better than yours."

"Why is that a good thing?" I asked.

Luke shrugged. Another fart blasted from Luke's Baby Bot's butt.

"Yo, I think you should change his diaper. That sounded kinda wet," Just Charles said.

Ben shook his head, disgusted. "I'm no longer in the mood for pizza."

"Ugh," Luke groaned, rolling off the bean bag chair and standing up.

I nodded to Luke. "Need help?"

"Yeah, that would be good."

"Ben, why don't you help Luke here?"

"I didn't offer any help," he said, simply. So much for all the support we would be giving each other.

Luke plucked the Baby Bot out of its container and placed it on the coffee table, a fresh diaper at the ready.

Luke opened up the diaper. "Ugh. This is disgusting." He tossed the diaper in the air. It soared over our heads and onto the floor on the other side of the couch.

"What are you doing?" I asked.

Derek ran down the stairs, grabbed the bannister, and swung around into the basement. "What the-" he yelled, nearly stepping in the devil's dung diaper.

"Dude, keep your baby's poop away from me." He picked it up and tossed it into our crowd.

We scattered like it was a hand grenade. Ben even flipped the coffee table over for cover, which meant the Baby Bot fell on its head.

We all held our breath, hoping it wouldn't start crying. Thankfully, it didn't budge.

It didn't make any sense. A mouse could fart in the next town over and the Baby Bot could wake up, but it falls on its head and nothing.

"What does it look like, by the way?" Derek asked.

"You haven't seen it?" I asked.

"No, I don't change diapers."

Just Charles said, "Dude, get with the program. Dudes can change diapers, too."

Derek shrugged. "It looks like poop. Does it smell?"

Luke leaned in and took a whiff. "Not that bad."

"Is it edible?"

"Why would you ask that?" I asked, disgusted.

Derek ignored me. "Try it. It looks like pudding."

"It's not pudding," Luke said.

"It's not really poop, though."

Derek and Luke continued to stare at the faux poo.

"Smell it again," Derek said.

The Baby Bot's butt exploded like a geyser. I took cover, not sure how far the poo would travel.

"Son of a-" Derek yelled.

I looked over to see both Derek and Luke with brown goo all over their faces, lips and mouth included.

Luke took the brunt of the hit. We all held our breath, not sure how he would react. I wasn't sure if he would pass out, smash up half the basement, or break down in tears.

He cocked his head, licked his lips, and said, "It doesn't taste that bad. I actually taste a hint of thyme in there. It could use a bit more salt, though."

"What the heck is thyme?" Derek asked, wiping his face with his t-shirt.

"Yeah, what the heck is that?" Ben asked.

"You're so uncivilized," Luke said, smugly.

I laughed. "You just ate baby poop. Who's the uncivilized one?"

Luke said, "I'm not gonna lie, this is better than the chocolate pudding in the cafeteria."

Even though Derek had wiped his face, the full depth of his butt chin was difficult to access, meaning he still had brown goop in his butt chin.

Luke laughed. "Dude, your face looks exactly like my baby's butt."

"Watch it, Lucas. Or I'll beat you so bad, you'll be wearing a diaper for the rest of your life."

Gulp.

THE NEXT DAY, I sat with the usual crew in lunch. I stared down at the day's lunch: beans and franks. I shook my head, bewildered. "How do you mess up beans and franks? It tastes like a rubber eraser."

Sophie looked over at me and asked, "What do we want our baby to be when he grows up?"

I thought for a moment. "Umm, you mean our fake baby?" I asked.

"If you treat him like a fake baby, we're gonna fail," Sophie said, annoyed.

Based on her level of annoyance, which was certainly at the stuck-in-traffic level, but seemingly not yet at the wheels-fell-off-the-car level, I decided to play along. "Okay," I said, thinking. "I want him to be a scientist, just like his dad, but I hope he never blows off his eyebrows. Randy's kid, maybe."

Of course, Randolph "R-Money" Warblemacher, was passing right behind me. "My kid will never blow off his eyebrows like an idiot. You know, like you, Davenfart."

I turned around. "That wasn't me. It was Flea," I said, my annoyance levels approaching wobbling wheels.

"It's a likely story. I didn't see Flea's eyebrows blow off."

"Whatever," I said. "He has strong eyebrows."

Randy responded, "No! You have weak eyebrows, Davenfart. And that sickens me."

"Randy, everything about you sickens me."

He scoffed and stormed off.

I didn't have the energy to deal with his idiocy. I was so tired by the end of the day, I could barely stand up. I waddled up to Ben and leaned on him as we made our way out of the building toward the buses.

"What's wrong?" Ben asked.

I didn't even look up. I groaned, "Life is meaningless. I feel like someone peed in my cornflakes."

"You don't even eat cornflakes."

"Why does that matter?" I asked. "I'd still be mad if someone peed in them. My feet are heavier. They're like giant bricks. I think my socks are made of concrete. And my arms. They're so heavy. I think they might fall off."

"Hurry up. We gotta catch the bus," Ben said.

I wasn't really paying attention. My nose was itchy, but I couldn't lift my arms. I had to get creative. I separated from Ben in search of itchy nose relief.

Ben looked over at me and said, "What the-"

"Ahhh," I said, rubbing my nose on the brick wall outside the school.

"What are you doing?"

"My nose is itchy and I can't lift my arms. Even my hair is tired."

"How is that even possible?" Ben asked.

"I don't know, but I can feel it. But Hairy Pitter is still good." He's my one armpit hair. I've been hoping for more, but no such luck. My brother has like a forest of it. I think he combs it. And he thinks I'm the dork.

~

I WOKE up from a nap that afternoon to my mother and Sophie staring at me. I jumped up off the den couch and nearly broke my ankle tripping over the coffee table.

"Ahhh, farts!" I said, hopping up and down, holding my ankle.

"Shhh," Sophie said. "You'll wake the baby."

I sat back down and fell into the couch, closing my eyes.

My mother chuckled.

"What? This is hard," I said. "I'm so tired."

My mother whispered, "You and your brother are cracking me up. Try doing this for three kids who are four years apart."

"Why would anyone do *that*? That's insane," I asked.

"That's what we did with you, your brother, and your sister."

"There's something wrong with you."

My mother smiled. "I'll leave you two alone." She left Sophie and me alone. Well, with the Baby Bot, too.

Sophie handed me some sort of flannel-patterned cloth. "I got this for you," she said, smiling.

I stared at it, trying to figure out what it was. My brain couldn't focus. My eyes just kept zooming in and out on the flannel pattern. "It's like an optical illusion," I said, mesmerized. "What's it for?"

"It's a sling," Sophie said.

"My arms are tired, but I'm not sure I need medical attention for it."

Sophie laughed. "It's not for you. It's for the baby."

"The baby has arm problems? We should probably send it back and hope they're shipping new ones from China. By bird. It'll arrive by the time we graduate."

"It's not for the baby's arms," Sophie said, annoyed. "It's to put the baby in so you can bond with it."

"Oh. Okay." It was kind of weird. I wasn't sure why I needed to bond with a plastic doll, but Sophie wasn't the kind of girl to argue with, especially since the doll arrived.

Sophie continued, "They say you bond better with the baby if you take your shirt off."

"Really? You want me to take my shirt off?" I shrugged. "Maybe Baby Bot will like to play with Hairy Pitter."

"Who the heck is that?"

"Never mind," I said, shaking my head. "I feel weird taking my shirt off in front of you."

"It's not a big deal. I've seen you in the pool."

"My parents will think it's weird."

Sophie said, simply, "It's only weird if you think it's weird."

I laughed nervously. "I do think it's weird."

"Just do it," Sophie pleaded.

"I'm not an athlete. That slogan doesn't motivate me."

Sophie said, "Just try it. Maybe it will boost our grade."

"Okay," I said. I pulled off my shirt and dropped it on the couch.

Thankfully, my mother walked back in. She stared at me, shocked.

My shoulders slumped. I just shook my head, as she raised eyebrow.

"Umm, everything okay in here?" my mother asked.

"Perfect, Mom. Just perfect."

10

The next day, we had a sub in science class. Ms. Kelvin was out sick. Flea and a couple of other kids were, too. The sub, Miss Froehlich, gave us a bunch of busy work. We had to read a chapter from the textbook and answer a few questions. I knew most of what was on there, so I finished it as quickly as I could and then put my head down for a nap. I was thankful for some good rest time.

I woke up to a nudge. "Dude. Dude. You're in my seat."

I lifted my head up and looked around. "Where am I?" I asked, the skinny boy staring at me.

"Science, dude. You okay?"

"Yeah, totally," I said, popping out of my seat. There's nothing like the fear of embarrassment giving you a little shot of energy.

The bell rang. "You better hurry," he said.

"Thanks," I said, slinging my backpack over my shoulder.

I hustled out of the science lab and slinked around corners. With the hallways empty, I was an easy target for

Principal Buthaire. He liked preying on innocent kids. After a few twists, turns, and hiding behind garbage pails, the exit doors were in sight. Energy surged through me, as victory was mine!

But then, I heard the familiar, much-despised, whiny voice of Prince Butt Hair behind me. "Misterrrr Davenport. Why am I not surprised?"

I turned around and took a deep breath, my shoulders slumping. I looked up at him. "Because you try to catch me being late every day?"

Principal Buthaire's shoulders slumped. "Not every day," he said, defensively. He tore off a detention slip, his smile returning. "But it does make my day. I should try more often."

More often? If I wasn't such a klutz, I would join ninja school or something. My stealthiness could use some fine tuning. I took my detention slip and slinked out the door, on my way to finish out my day at the middle school.

I entered an empty Atrium, too late to catch any of my friends before Advisory started. I looked around ghost town, in a haze. I did a double take after noticing an empty, cozy-looking bench under one of the dogwood trees.

"What's the big deal if I just grab a quick nap during Advisory?" I asked myself out loud.

"It's not a big deal at all, Austin. Not. At. All. The bell for first period will wake you up."

"You really are a genius."

"Thank you, my boy. You're pretty sharp, yourself. And handsome, even if you don't have the family butt chin."

"Wow. You're too kind. I've always been self-conscious about that. I have to say, it's been a real pleasure speaking with you this morning."

"Likewise."

I was on the verge of delirium. Or I was just really interesting to talk to. You decide.

I headed over to the bench and lay down across it. I used my backpack as a pillow. Before my head hit the comfy pile of hardcover books, I was asleep.

AS YOU PROBABLY CAN IMAGINE, I woke up to laughter. The refreshing sensation I got from that fabulous ten-minute nap vanished into thin air, as I opened my eyes to see my principal, Ms. Pierre, staring at me, quite disapprovingly.

"Good morning, Misterrrr Davenport," Principal Armpit Hair said, devoid of emotion. "Do you care to explain why you're sleeping on this bench during school?"

I did not care to explain it, but I felt like she would not accept my silence on the matter. "Umm, well, I was exhausted from the Baby Bots."

Before Ms. Pierre could answer, Nick DeRozan walked by and said, "Nice mustache, Davenport."

Mustache? What the heck was he talking about? I sat up and instinctively reached for my upper lip. There was nothing there.

Ms. Pierre stood up and handed me a detention slip. "Don't cut Advisory again, Misterrrr Davenport."

As soon as Armpit Hair walked away, Ben rushed over.

"Dude, nice mustache," he said, trying to hold in laughter.

"What are you talking about?" I asked, annoyed.

"Somebody must've drawn a magic marker mustache on you while you were sleeping."

Randy walked by with Regan and said, "Why did you do that, Davenfart? You'll hit puberty in ten years. Maybe."

"I have armpit hair!" I yelled, for reasons I don't understand. "Well, one, but Hairy Pitter is the wizard of armpit hairs!" I also don't understand why I said that.

Sophie walked up. She did a double take when she saw me. "What the heck happened?"

"I'm a man, baby," I said.

Sophie rolled her eyes. "No, seriously."

I shrugged. "I fell asleep on the bench. How bad is it?"

Sophie took out a mirror from her pocketbook and showed me.

"Yeah, it's pretty bad. I think handlebars would've been cooler. Can you power wash my face?" I asked Ben.

Derek passed by and said, "Yeah, please. Anything has to be an improvement over that."

"We can't all have the family butt chin, butt face boy!" I yelled.

I was cracking up. I needed help.

So, apparently, there were kids who thought it was cool to have a boorish Baby Bot and wanted to parade them around. Seemingly half the eighth grade decided to meet up at the local mall with their Baby Bots to hang out and annoy every other patron with hysterically-crying robot babies.

I was there, too, minding my own business, walking down the hallway of the mall with Sophie, Ben, and Sammie when I had the pleasure of bumping into Randy and Regan. They were with Nick DeRozan, Derek, and a few others. I fed Baby Bot as we walked.

Randy's voice boomed into my ears, singing, "Our baby is better than yours."

I stepped away from him and turned, confused.

Randy continued talking, "He sleeps through the night." He looked down at the Baby Bot in the stroller and said, "Isn't that right, Joonie Woonie."

"Joonie Woonie?" I laughed.

Regan chimed in, "For Randy Junior."

I was tired of his nonsense. Tired of robot babies. Just plain tired. I looked Randy dead in the eyes and said, "Your baby stinks."

Randy scoffed, "Don't talk to our baby like that."

"I wasn't talking to your baby. I was talking to you," I said.

"You wanna talk to my fists?" Randy said, stepping toward me, menacingly.

"You can't hit me, you idiot. I'm holding a baby! Everybody knows that," I said, hoping that it was true.

Derek chimed in, unhelpfully, as always, "I'll hold it for you."

"That's very kind of you, bro, but I don't trust you with my baby. I recall you throwing yours like a football across the den."

"You did what?" Derek's partner, **Toni Amira, shrieked.** "You said it was an accident."

"Yeah, it was an accident. It wasn't supposed to bounce off the couch."

Thankfully, Randy Junior started crying. It was the first time the Baby Bots actually helped me.

Randy picked Junior up out of the stroller. "I'm the best father in the world," he said to no one in particular. He looked at Junior. "If you should have the horrible luck of growing up with a Davenfart, you must make it your mission to crush the nerdy turd every chance you get."

"Nerdy turd. I like that," Derek said.

Sophie grabbed my arm. "Let's go. We don't need to waste our time with these clowns."

"Thanks for the help, as always," I said to Derek, as I walked past.

"I'm warning you, Davenfart!" Randy called out.

I had no idea what he was warning me about, and I didn't care to stick around, so we just took off down the hall.

"He's such a clown," I said.

"Totally," Ben agreed.

Sammie looked at Sophie and said, "Did you see those baby bottles Regan had in the diaper bag? I totally want those."

"Why are you gonna waste money on that stuff?" I asked.

The girls ignored me. "I saw them at Babies R Us. Why don't we go check them out?"

I whispered to Ben. "Are you thinking what I'm thinking?"

"Yes. Let's get tacos," he said.

"That's not what I was thinking, but it's not a bad idea. I was thinking that maybe Randy's baby might like to try something other than baby formula."

"You're gonna pee in the bottle?" Ben asked, a little too loud.

"No," I whispered. "I was thinking energy drinks."

"We couldn't!"

"But pee is okay?"

"Good point," he said. "Are you sure?"

"It's not a real baby. It's a demon robot and it deserves that and more," I said.

THE GIRLS ENDED up buying the bottles. It took some coaxing, but they agreed to let us get some man time, so we could pick up tacos, as long as we agreed not to complain about all the baby stuff they were buying. Luke was able to slip a bottle out of Sammie's bag when she wasn't looking, so we had the delivery device. We just needed the energy.

I stood in front of a small food and drink kiosk with the guys, staring at drink options, particularly energy drinks.

"Red Bull?" Ben asked.

"Nah, I like bulls," I said.

Luke said, "Rock Star?"

"Really?" I asked. Randy and I had gone head to head in a battle of the bands competition a while back. Perhaps you remember that story. I couldn't believe he would ask that.

"Sorry. You're right."

I opened the door to the refrigerator and said, "Monster."

"Yes, please," Ben said, excitedly.

"This is perfect." I admired it for a minute before heading to the cash register.

$3 later, we huddled together, as I poured the can of caffeine into the Baby Bot bottle. If I wasn't such a nice kid, I might've let out an evil cackle.

As I tightened the lid, I asked, "Where do you think they are?" I was usually trying to avoid Randy, not find him.

"This place is huge," Ben said.

"They were heading toward Urban Outfitters before," Luke said.

"That was half an hour ago," I countered. "I got it," I said. I pulled out my phone and texted Derek, 'Where are you? Meeting Dad soon.'

A few minutes later, Derek responded, 'Outside some stupid furniture store.'

"Oh, God. I think Randy and Regan are shopping for baby furniture. This is going too far."

Thankfully, the girls weren't with us. I imagined Sophie and Sammie shrieking, "Cribs! We need those!"

We trekked through the mall, eventually making it to the furniture store. My brother was nowhere to be found, so I hoped they hadn't moved on. We strolled in and began the stealth search. I wasn't sure how we would slip the imposter baby bottle into their diaper bag without being detected, but we would figure that out when the time came.

It didn't take us long to find them. Randy and Regan were not actually shopping for baby furniture. They were standing in front of a giant ten-foot mirror, admiring themselves while holding the baby.

"They're unbelievable," I whispered. "Let's slip it in the diaper bag before they see us."

"Good idea," Ben said.

I slinked over to the stroller and diaper bag, which were behind them, off to the side next to a dresser. I flipped open the diaper bag while reaching around the side of the dresser, out of sight.

And then an obnoxious, bearded salesman came over, his belly arriving a full three seconds before the rest of him, bumping into everything and making a racket. "You guys gonna buy anything or just stare at yourselves all day?" he said to Randy and Regan, annoyed. "This isn't Harry Potter's Mirror of Erised."

"And what do you know about it, Hagrid?" Randy asked, even more annoyed, eyeing him through the mirror.

I flipped the bag shut, not sure if Randy or Regan saw me. I rolled to my left, nearly knocked over a plant, and crawled around a few pieces of furniture before I was able to stand up and walk normally out of the store.

I couldn't contain myself. When I met the rest of my crew outside, I walked excitedly up to Ben, my hand readied for a high five. I yelled, "Boom, baby!" Our hands surged forward, nowhere close to crossing paths. Our pinkies intermingled and pulled. I thought I heard something pop. One of us might've cried like a Baby Bot. Or both of us.

11

The next Monday at school didn't start off so well. I hadn't heard anything about Randy Junior and his baby bottle. As soon as I walked into the Atrium and met my friends, that time came.

Randy walked up to us. He was so angry, he was shaking. Plus, he also yelled, "I'm so angry!"

"What's the matter?" I asked, faking surprise.

"You swapped Randy Jr.'s formula and poisoned my baby! He nearly died!"

"It's a doll, psycho," I said. "And how do you know it was even me?"

"I dusted for fingerprints," he said, simply.

"You what? How do you know what my fingerprints look like?"

"I have them on file for moments exactly like this. That's a low blow, Davenfart. Even for you!"

I was pretty certain he had the two of us confused. He was the King of Low Blows. "So, maybe I did. What are you gonna do about it?" I asked. It was a stupid question.

Randy grabbed my doll out of its stroller by its hair and

pulled. I surged forward like a lion on the prowl, but Randy pushed me back with his other hand. I fell to the ground with a thud, as Randy took two big steps and drop kicked the doll across the Atrium. It soared over the boys' tennis team, the girls' softball team, and the reed section of the band. "It's long and it...is...far!" Randy yelled.

Nick DeRozan's voice boomed, "The kick is good!"

The doll smacked into the wall with a sickening crack. I ran after it, hoping to catch it, but of course, I was nowhere close. I did knock over a garbage can, Jasmine Jane, and the Teriaka twins.

"What's going on here?" Mr. Muscalini asked, fists on his hips.

I ran over to Mr. Muscalini, pointing to Randy. "He punted my Baby Bot! You can't punt another kid's Baby Bot! That has to be in the rules somewhere, doesn't it?"

"Warblemacher! Get over here!"

Randy walked over, tentatively.

Finally! Randy was going to get what he deserved.

"That was a pretty good punt, Warblemacher. Why have you been holding out on me? We could've beaten the Bisons with a boot like that."

I interrupted. "Sir? I think the important point here is that he punted my baby and it's going to cause me to fail."

"No, I don't think that was the point at all. Gopher football comes before your grades, Davenport."

Ahhh, farts.

12

So, Sammie had a great idea for Friday night. It was to take our Baby-cyborgs out for a walk and then have sushi. She was taking this whole parenting thing too far. I don't understand how all of a sudden, you could be too mature for pizza. Who the heck outgrows cheese? True, stuff can grow on your cheese and it might smell kinda funky, but it's not biologically possible to outgrow cheese. I've studied the science in depth.

But Ben was in trouble with Sammie. Sophie and I were on a relationship roller-coaster ride, while Just Charles and Cheryl were on the brink of disaster. Luke and Ditzy Dayna, while not dating, were totally fine. Go figure.

The girls walked behind us as we pushed the strollers.

"Let's just hurry this up so we can eat," I said.

"Agreed," Ben said, speeding up. "But sushi? Sammie is too sophisticated for me, man."

"Dude, watch you're stroller, man. Stay in your lane," I said.

"You stay in your lane," Ben shot back.

"I am," I said. "This is me not staying in my lane." I

swerved the stroller left toward Ben, and took it a little too far. The front wheel of my stroller collided with his.

"Dude! You're gonna wake the baby!" Ben screamed, swerving his stroller back toward me, but harder.

I attempted countermeasures, but, surprisingly, my reflexes weren't quick enough. Ben's stroller slammed into mine, t-boning it. The girls shrieked from behind us. Or maybe that was me. My stroller tipped sideways from the momentum of the crash. I jerked it back to center it, but surprisingly, used too much strength, and overcorrected, tossing the baby into the air. It soared over Ben's stroller, as we both ran toward my Baby Bot that was log-rolling in the air.

"No!" I yelled, pushing Ben's stroller to the side, unfortunately, launching Ben's Baby Bot into the air as well.

Nerds juggling. It was not a sporting event that typically ended well. Ben heard the commotion behind him and turned back. His eyes widened. He stepped toward me, his arms outstretched for his own Baby Bot, while mine was plummeting to the ground behind him. I tried to sidestep him, but I tripped over his feet, which wasn't as hurtful as you might think. It propelled me forward. I reach for the Baby Bot. It was the best trip of my life, not including Hawaii.

Sophie yelled, "Our baby!"

I yelled, "I got this, baby!"

My body stretched to its limits, as I went horizontal. I felt the Baby Bot's plastic butt fall into my outstretched hands. I squeezed those buns as hard as I could, praying that I would finally catch something and save the day. Even though I was highly responsible for the Baby Bot's unfortunate flight, but let's not focus on that.

I had a flashback of my performance in the school

musical when I tried to catch a flying doll across the stage and failed miserably. I also almost burned down the place, which was not my finest moment, either. My eyes closed, as my body hit the ground with a thud. I tasted dirt, grass, and perhaps Mrs. Shikadance's poodle's piddle. It didn't matter. I opened my eyes, not sure if my hands were deceiving me.

Sophie and Sammie cheered. I had caught the Baby Bot! Energy surged through my body like I had just chugged a dozen cups of coffee (don't try that at home, kids). I popped up, a huge smile across my face. Sophie ran toward me, her arms outstretched.

"You did it! You finally did it!" she yelled.

I tossed the Baby Bot to the side and engulfed Sophie in a giant hug. We nearly toppled over. And then it hit me. I had just thrown the Baby Bot onto the street. And, right on cue, it started to cry.

"Oh, my God! What did you do?" Sophie asked, concerned.

"I was so excited, I must've put it down. Gently."

Sophie let go of me and hurried over to the Baby Bot that lay face down on the street, leaning up against the curb. She picked up the Baby Bot and looked at it. Her face dropped.

"What's wrong?" Sammie asked.

"His head! My baby has a scar!"

Ben and I stared at each other. I walked over to take a closer look. My Baby Bot had a jagged gash in its plastic head that ran pretty deep. I held my breath, knowing that Sophie would be mad. I just wasn't sure how mad.

"I...Can't...Believe...You...Did...That."

"Oops?" I said.

"Oops?" Sophie asked, aggressively.

"Yeah, it was an accident. But here's the good news," I

said, making it up as I went, which was pretty typical of me, I guess. "That scar looks like a lightning bolt. We've got the only Harry Potter Baby Bot. I think we should name him Harry or maybe even the Chosen One."

Sophie's eyes bored into me.

"It's negotiable," I said. "How about the Boy Who Lived?"

"You should be concerned about whether or not you're a boy who lives," Sophie said, shaking.

Gulp.

So, social time with the girls was over for obvious reasons. They were both fuming mad. The only good news was that they took the Baby Bots with them and I didn't have to eat raw fish just to pretend I was all mature and stuff. The boys and I ordered pizza from Frank's. We were all still struggling with our bundles of Baby Bot, so it turned into a venting session.

"Why do we even have to do this?" I asked. "We're still babies ourselves!"

"Just Charles still wets his bed," Luke said.

"Do not!"

"That's questionable. What's that squishy pad underneath your covers?" Luke asked with an eyebrow raised.

"I have allergies," Just Charles said, defensively.

"And a leaky bladder," Ben said, laughing.

Apparently, Luke had touched a nerve. Just Charles countered, "Your mother still cuts your food."

"No, she doesn't!"

My phone dinged with a text. It was Sophie. Uh, oh. It read, 'You're still taking the baby overnight.'

'Okay. I'm looking forward to it.'

'Right.'

"I can't win," I said, tossing my phone on the couch. "Even when I pretend that I care, I don't get any credit."

"Maybe you should care," Just Charles said.

"Since when do you care? And why should I care about an evil robot? I mean, I care about R2-D2 and BB-8, but that nightmare? And speaking of nightmares, how am I gonna get sleep?"

"Get a babysitter," Ben said.

"I have sixteen dollars," I said.

My sister, Leighton, came downstairs and grabbed a slice of pizza.

"You're welcome," I said, as she was walking back toward the stairs, not having said a word to us.

"I'll thank Dad, who paid for it," she said.

I asked, "Hey, fabulous sister, will you watch my baby tonight?"

"What's in it for me?"

"Sixteen dollars?"

Leighton chuckled. "I can get freshman to give me sixteen dollars just to walk down the hall with them."

"How much then?" I asked. I didn't have any more money, but I would figure it out to get a night off and some rest.

"A hundred."

I shrieked, "A hundred? After all I do for you?"

"Which is what? Be annoying? You should pay me for that, too."

"How much do I owe you?" I asked, stupidly.

"Twenty bucks," she said.

"I only have sixteen."

"That'll do."

ON THE BUS the next morning, I noticed how peaceful the hum of the bus could be. I just let my mind go, becoming one with the hum. And then I was jolted awake, yet again.

I looked side to side, spraying drool in every direction, like an old dog. A gob of it splattered onto the window.

"Austin...Austin!"

"Huh? What?" I looked around, trying to get my bearings. Barn Door was staring at me. "Where are we?" I asked.

"High school. Where we go every morning."

"That makes sense in a world that makes little sense. Sorry about that Barn," I said, wiping my mouth.

"Don't worry about it. I remember what it was like."

"How did you handle it?" I asked, as we exited the bus.

"I had a nervous breakdown and got a doctor's note to get out of it."

"Hmmmm. That's an interesting strategy," I said, gripping my chin. "What kind of things did you do?"

"I lost a chunk of my hair. I stopped eating. I started losing time. I woke up at three in the morning, holding my grandmother in the Camel Clutch."

"That's good stuff, man. I think I can do something with that," I said, my weakened brain swirling for ideas.

"I'm glad my breakdown might be useful for you," Barn Door said, with a clap of my shoulder.

Had any of my other friends said that, I would wonder if they were being sarcastic, but Barney seemingly meant it.

I SAT with Luke in history. Dr. Dinkledorf, one of my favorite teachers, hadn't arrived yet, so we were all just talking.

"You're not gonna believe what Lit Fart did," Luke said, excitedly.

"Lit Fart? What are you talking about?" I asked.

"It's who I'm talking about. Dayna and I named the baby Lit Fart."

"What? Are you serious?"

"Yep. I love it," Luke said.

"Why?"

"Because it's awesome and you never let me name the band that."

I shook my head. "Because it stinks. No pun intended. What did Ditzy Dayna say?"

"I told her that two Hollywood stars just named their kids the same thing and she was cool with it."

Just then Dr. Dinkledorf arrived with Ditzy Dayna and a few others.

"Take your seats, please," Dr. Dinkledorf said. He almost tripped over Lit Fart's baby carrier. "Geez, Louise!" he said, stumbling. "This is getting out of hand." He regrouped and said, "When my son, Thaddeus, was born-"

Ditzy Dayna interrupted, "Did they have hospitals when he was born?"

"Yes! How old do you think I am?" he scoffed.

Jay Parnell asked, "How old is Yoda?"

"Nine hundred!" Dr. Dinkledorf boomed.

"Yeah, so like that old," Regan said.

"Did Yoda have kids?" Ditzy Dayna asked.

"He was a Jedi father to all," Dr. Dinkledorf said, regrouping.

I was impressed with his Star Wars knowledge. Most teachers wouldn't know how old Yoda was. It was one of the reasons he was one of my favorite teachers.

Ditzy Dayna said, "I thought you knew so much about history because you lived through it all."

Dr. Dinkledorf took a deep breath and muttered, "I need to retire."

DEREK RIFLED through the fridge drawers in the kitchen, as I packed up my backpack. I overheard my father say, "I mean, I guess we could sell the house and get something bigger."

Derek emerged from the fridge with a chocolate pudding. Oh, great. I couldn't wait to see how that looks in his butt chin. He chimed in to the conversation he was not a part of, "Yeah, I want my own suite and a batting cage. Full-length basketball court. Put that on the requirements."

I had no idea where Leighton even was, but her voice echoed, "I want a makeup studio."

I didn't even know what we were talking about, but I stuck my head into the den and said, "I want a science lab."

Derek bumped my shoulder as he walked by. "Dork."

"Guys, this is a parents' only discussion," my dad said.

"There's no such thing in this house," Derek said.

My mother smirked and said, "Apparently."

I sat down on the couch next to my mother and across from my father. "Wait, are you really thinking about moving? Are we gonna be in a different school? I don't want to leave my friends."

"Yeah, it might be tough for Austin to make two friends somewhere else. And God knows, there won't be another Sophie wherever we go," Derek said.

"Shut up, Derek."

"Boys. We're not leaving the area. We…thought it might

be nice to have a little more space now that you're all... getting bigger," my dad said, eyeing my mother.

Leighton called in, "Hey! Do you think I'm fat?"

"You're perfect, honey," my mother said.

"Except for her hairy back," Derek said.

"I don't have a hairy back!"

I tried to be supportive. "It's not a big deal, sis. It's kinda cool these days to date werewolves. It's like in every book." I looked at Derek. "Do you know what those are?"

"Funny, runt."

"Boys, enough," mom said, firmly.

"This has been fun," my dad said, standing up. "I have to go shave Leighton's back."

"Dad!"

So, you may remember that I once pretended I was sick so that I could skip school. There was fake puke, a lot of acting, and one unconvinced mother. Despite that, I was going to give it another go. This time, I was going with the Barn Door approach. My mental health was at stake and I needed a break. Perhaps even a soothing coma.

I moped into the kitchen before breakfast.

"Good morning," my mother said.

"Hello, Mr. Shikadance," I said, with a nod.

"Mr. Shikandance? He's been dead for years. Are you okay?" She walked over to me and felt my head.

"It has been a long time. It's good to see you again." I wobbled and grabbed the chair, steadying myself.

"Serious, is something wrong? Sit down. I'll make you breakfast."

"Mom, is that you?" I asked. "I think I lost time." I sat down. "I should probably take the day off."

"Okay," she said. "I'll take you to the hospital after breakfast."

"Hospital?" I gulped. "Umm, why don't we see how I respond to some rest?"

"Are you a doctor now? Do you know how serious it is to lose time? You thought I was Mr. Shikadance. I know I haven't been keeping up with my normal routine, but the guy was like a hundred years old. My skin's not that bad. Maybe we should get your vision checked, too."

I didn't know how to respond. I wasn't sure if she was onto me or really concerned.

She picked up the phone.

"What are you doing?" I asked.

"Calling for an ambulance," she said, simply.

"Maybe I should just get some sleep. It's too early," I said.

"Are you really losing time?" she asked, staring into my eyes.

I couldn't look at her. "No," I said.

"So, what's going on?"

"This stupid Baby Bot is going to end me."

"Sorry, honey. That's part of the test. You're just going to have to deal with it."

"Mom, please! My mental health is at stake. You don't know what it's like!"

"Yeah, I kinda do. I raised three of you."

"Well, you didn't do a good job, because I can't handle this," I said, feeling kind of bad for saying it.

"Oh, is that so?" my mother asked, offended.

"Maybe," I said, unsurely.

"Have a great day at school!" she said, cheerfully.

"Come on, Mom!"

"Sorry, buddy. I'm a bad parent," she said, shrugging.

"I guess I deserved that."

I SAT in home ec and health with Luke. We were pretty early, so there were just a few kids and Mrs. Flaum. She walked over to Luke and me.

"How's it going with the Baby Bots, boys?" Mrs. Flaum asked.

"Umm, there's room for improvement," Luke said.

"Any tips on how we can get through this?" I asked.

She chuckled. "Well, first of all, you need a better mindset. It's not about getting through it. You have to embrace the parenting process. Have you named your baby?"

"Lit Fart," Luke said.

"Little Fart?"

"No, that would be ridiculous. It's Lit Fart, like when you hold a lighter up to your butt and fart."

"I've never done that and I don't recommend it. Do you know a kid named Flea? He's a football player in high school."

"Yeah, I've heard of him," Luke said.

"I'm friends with him. He's my lab partner in science," I added.

"Well, he tried that on Taco Tuesday and nearly burned the place down. That dude can eat a lot of tacos. Let's just leave it at that," she said.

I wished we had left it a lot sooner. And then the Speaker of Doom crackled. "Mrs. Flaum, please send Austin Davenport to the main office to see Ms. Pierre."

"Ugh," I said. "What now?" I looked at Luke and said, "I'll be back. Probably with detention."

I grabbed my stuff and headed down to the main office, my brain searching for a reason for the summons. I pulled open the door to the bustling office, my home away from home. I'd rather have a place at the beach, but whatever.

Mrs. Murphy saw the somber look on my face and said, "Don't worry. You're not in trouble."

"Huh?" I asked. "Is it April Fool's Day?"

"Nope," Mrs. Murphy said, chuckling.

Mrs. Murphy opened the door to the Arm Pit. I walked in and plopped into the chair across from Ms. Pierre.

I was so weary, the cushy chair seemed like it could be a nice spot for a nap, although I didn't want to get detention again. I took a deep breath, as I always did, not sure why I was there.

"Hmm. This place smells nice for an arm pit," I said, stupidly.

"Excuse me?" Ms. Pierre asked, pointedly.

Ahhh, farts. "Ummm, you know, the school is like a giant armpit because kids never use deodorant."

"I'm sure Mr. Zorch would be pleased to hear that."

"It's not his fault. There's only so much body spray and Fabreze can do."

"This conversation smells," Randy said, entering the room.

"Misterrr Warblemacher, sit down," Ms. Pierre said.

Randy did as he was told.

"I've received a complaint that you forcefully took Mr. Davenport's Baby Bot and punted it across the Atrium. What do you have to say to these accusations?"

Randy fidgeted. "I dropped the baby by mistake and tried to cushion his fall with my foot."

Typical Randy. Lying through his teeth. My voice rose three octaves. "The baby soared over three groups of people and nearly dented the wall. Had the baby not had a plasti-cally-reinforced head, we might be at a funeral right now," I said, flabbergasted.

"I'm very strong. Mr. Muscalini has me on extra protein."

"This is unbelievable," I said, slumping in my chair.

Ms. Armpit Hair said, "Witnesses say that it was intentional, Mr. Warblemacher. You will have one week's detention!"

I thrust my fists in the air. "Praise the Lord! Finally!"

"Misterrrr Davenport, that is hardly appropriate behavior. You will join him for detention for two of those days."

"For what?" I questioned, annoyed.

"The lack of separation of church and state," Ms. Armpit Hair said, simply.

"Huh?"

"You broke the law. You're lucky you're not going to jail."

I was pretty certain that I hadn't broken any laws, but arguing with Ms. Armpit Hair or Prince Butt Hair rarely ended on a positive note for me. And my lawyer was terrible, anyway. The last time I had one in front of the school board, it was a disaster.

I STOOD at the edge of a grassy meadow. Tall, wild flowers arced in the breeze. And then I saw her. Sophie, my angel, floating down from the sky. I ran toward her, taking in the plethora of spring scents, as my love soared toward me, her lips puckered and lined up to mine.

And then I felt an earthquake rumble. I turned around, not sure what was going on, barely keeping my footing. I looked back into the sky, but Sophie was gone. Ahhh, farts!

"Austin! Austin! Wake up," my mother said, shaking my shoulder. "You need to get moving."

I opened my eyes to see reality. It was 6:40 A.M. I was late for school. The last thing I needed was to go from my dreams of Sophie to a nightmare of detention with Prince

Butt Hair. I'm pretty certain he waits for me, detention pass at the ready, salivating.

"If you hurry, you might still be able to catch the bus."

I hopped out of bed and headed to the bathroom. It was empty, which was so uncommon, I thought I might still be dreaming. Perhaps I could still catch the bus. I took the fastest shower ever. I didn't even wait for the water to heat up, which gave me a little extra jolt of energy. I surged out of the bathroom, a towel wrapped around my waist.

Derek turned the corner, heading for the bathroom. As we crossed paths, he tugged at my towel and said, "Thanks." He wasn't in high school science like his genius brother, so he got to sleep later and didn't have to compete with Leighton for the shower, which is like an Olympic sport. The next year was going to be horrific with all three of us in high school together.

"Dude!" I yelled, as he laughed. My buns were bare for the whole world to see. Well, just my family, but still.

Leighton stuck her head into the hall. "Austin, are you... gross! I don't need to see your butt."

I hustled into my room and said, "You don't seem to complain about all the butts on everyone's faces around here."

I closed the door and got dressed as quickly as I could. Jeans. Batman t-shirt. I rocked it. I hustled out into the hallway.

"Adios!" Leighton yelled, closing the door behind her.

I grabbed my backpack, tore open the door, and rushed out, calling out, "Bye, Mom!"

I hopped down the steps, the cold ground permeating my sneakers. My sneakers! I looked down, realizing I was in my socks. In the distance, I heard the familiar screeching sound of the bus.

No! I rushed back inside, slipped on my sneakers, which were now annoyingly wet, and headed back out to see the bus hurdling down the street, too far for a nerd like me to catch up to with my athletic prowess. Or lackthereof.

My mother dropped me at school. The hallways were empty as I entered. Well, there was one familiar face there.

"Misterrrrr Davenport. Late again," Principal Buthaire said with an annoying smile.

"Yes, sir. I am," I said, simply.

"No witty comebacks? No excuses?" Prince Butt Hair asked, surprised.

"No, sir. I'm late."

He cocked his head to the side. "Are you sick? Are you dying, or something?"

"No, sir. It just feels like I am."

"Good. I'm glad you're not dying."

"You don't want me dead?" I asked surprised.

"I fear you would become more powerful than I could ever imagine."

I furrowed my brow. "Sir, I'm not Obi-wan Kenobi."

"Who?"

It figures that he wouldn't know Star Wars. "Never mind, sir."

"You will serve detention this afternoon," he said with a smile.

"Ok." I was already serving detention for Armpit Hair, so it was no big deal. Because I couldn't skip eighth period and go back to the high school for detention, Principal Buthaire outsourced it to the middle school. I took the pass and moped to science class.

14

Ben was over at my house. We had laundry to do for homework. We had no idea what we were doing. We stood in the laundry room, staring down at the pile of clothes scattered inside the washing machine.

"How much soap are we supposed to put in?" I asked.

Ben examined the detergent bottle. "I don't know. This stuff is written so tiny. Where's the cap? My mother just fills the cap and dumps it in."

"It's broken. My brother threw it at me and it cracked," I said.

"Typical," Ben said. "How dirty is all that stuff?"

"I don't know. Pretty dirty. Our gym clothes are in there. There's a lot of fear mixed into that fabric. It's gotta suck up extra soap," I said, scratching my head.

"I think you're right. We need extra soap to get the fear out. And can you really make something too clean?"

"Of course not. Just put a ton in. Better to have too much than too little, right?" I asked.

"Definitely." Ben turned the bottle of detergent over and

smiled, as the detergent glugged out of the bottle and onto the fear-filled clothes.

"We're gonna get extra credit for this being the cleanest load of laundry. Ever," I said, confidently.

We would not be getting extra credit. And we learned that you *can* have too much soap. We probably should've known from that crazy time when we saved the dance by turning it into a foam party with a boatload of soap. Unfortunately, we would not be the heroes in this one.

As Ben and I played FIFA on Playstation, waiting for the laundry to be done, Derek's voice boomed, "Mom! Austin blew up the laundry room!"

I had no idea what he was talking about, but the first rule of arguing with a sibling is to deny whatever it was your sibling just said. I called back, "I did not!"

I heard my mother say, "Oh, my...What the..." And then her voice echoed through the house, "Austin! What did you do? Get over here now!"

"Aaaahhh, farts," I said, not sure what happened.

I hurried to the laundry room with Ben at my heels. I stopped in the doorway and wondered how I would blame what I saw on Ben or perhaps Derek. The four of us just looked at the laundry room that was filled with soapy bubbles from top to bottom.

"What did you do?" My mother asked again.

"Well, we just wanted to wash the ceiling?" I said.

"You're so grounded," Derek said.

"I'll handle this, but thank you, Derek," my mother said.

"He should be grounded," Derek said, walking away.

"Shut your butt-chinned face," I whispered.

My mother asked, "How much soap did you use?"

"Umm, all of it?" I said, shrugging. "You can't be too clean. That's my motto, anyway."

My mother just shook her head and laughed.

"Can you make sure to sign my homework before you forget?" I asked.

"What was your homework?"

"Doing the laundry," I said, looking at my feet.

MRS. FLAUM STOOD in the front of our home ec and health class with her grade book in hand. "Well, I have to say that I'm a little disappointed with what the grades look like so far. There are some groups that I'm very proud of. Randy and Regan have done a fabulous job. They're in the top spot with an A+. Nick and Tammie, great improvement."

Randy looked over at me and smirked. I rolled my eyes and looked back at Mrs. Flaum.

"Who's at the bottom?" Regan asked.

"In need of the most improvement, Benjamin and Samantha, Luke and Dayna, and Austin and Sophie."

Randy and his crew chuckled, as they looked over at us.

Sophie looked over at me, disappointed. Neither of us liked to do poorly in school. It did not happen often.

I needed to change the subject. "How is it possible that Nick improved so much and that Randy and Regan are the only ones getting A's?" Nick was not overly nurturing or intelligent, unless he was nurturing a dodge ball into your face. He was very intelligent at doing that.

Even my brother was surprised. When we were at dinner later that night, he asked, "Why do you think Randy and Nick are the only ones who are passing home ec? Their bragging is getting really annoying." Derek didn't like to lose. And certainly not to Randy. They were frenemies, constantly competing for the sports spotlight.

I shrugged. "They've figured out the Baby Bot, I guess."

"Randy, I can understand, but Nick? Something is going on."

"I don't know," I said, cleaning up my plate. I headed into the den and plopped onto the couch.

I was determined to get something right. I had never failed a subject in school. Ever. Not even gym. True, Mr.

Muscalini passed us out of pity, but still. It's not my fault I wasn't born with gym genes.

I GRABBED MY PHONE. How could I beat the Baby Bot? I couldn't get it to sleep or stop crying. I certainly couldn't get it to stop projectile vomiting. What was I good at? Snarky humor. Yes, you're right, but I didn't know how to use it in that situation. I was good at learning. Research. Making connections. How could I use that? It hit me. The Internet and social media.

I Googled my butt off. I set up lists and alerts on Twitter and Instagram for every possible hashtag that could even come close to resembling Baby Bot 2000 with the hopes that people would start posting tips and hacks. And then I sat back and waited. And waited. Nothing. Nobody knew anything, other than that they hated Baby Bot 2000 and wished it had never been invented.

And then my stupid Baby Bot started crying.

"Please, somebody help me!" I said, frustrated. I picked it up out of its container and pat it on the back, still wailing.

My dad walked in. "Do you know the Bob and Shush?"

"I don't know anyone named Bob," I said, annoyed.

"No," he said, chuckling. "It's a baby-calming method. You bob up and down while shushing. Try it."

I bent my knees up and down while shushing quietly.

"That's it," my dad said. "I should patent this move."

I continued for a minute until the baby started to calm down. I looked at my dad, a smile breaking out on my face.

And then Derek had to go and ruin it all. He walked into the den and tossed his Baby Bot on the couch. It hit the cushion and sprung into the air, and onto the floor with a thud, landing on its head. The Babybeast started to wail. And then my Baby Bot joined his.

Derek plopped onto the couch. "Dude, can you shut my baby up?"

"No. I have my own baby to take care of," I said, looking at my dad.

"Well, I'm not doin' it," Derek said.

"Then fail," I said, in between bobbing and shushing.

My dad said, "Just do the Bob and Shush."

"I don't bob," Derek said, crossing his arms.

DESPITE LEARNING the Bob and Shush, which worked a little bit, it was clear to me that I needed a break. In the absence of a permanent break from Baby Bot, I at least needed a nap. Having gotten a twelve on my last science test, skipping science probably wasn't a great idea, but I didn't think I would retain much information, anyway.

I got the bathroom pass from Miss Kelvin and headed over to Max's. I barely had the strength to push open the door.

"Aus, what's up?" Max said, excited to see me.

"Dude, please tell me you have napping facilities. And do you happen to know how to change a diaper?"

"Of course. When I was back at Cherry Avenue, I used to offer group and one-on-one tutoring."

"I need some help," I said, nearly teetering over from exhaustion.

"Green smoothie with some caffeine?"

"Please," I said.

Max stepped closer. "Coming right up. Now, onto the baby issue. Do you know the Bob and Shush?"

"Yeah, my dad taught it to me. He says it's his patented move."

"The heck it is. I've got a patent pending on that. Every time someone calms their baby with a Bob and Shush, they're gonna have to pay me a dollar," Max said, confidently.

My brain was far from its highest capacity, but I was pretty certain Max was mistaken. "Yeah, that doesn't sound right."

Max called out toward the bathroom stall, "Hey, Michael. Can you come out here?"

I was so confused. Some dude emerged from one of the stalls. He was dressed in a suit with slicked back hair.

"Who the heck is that?" I asked. I had been through so many crazy scenarios with Max, I didn't know why I got surprised each time.

Max looked at me like it was totally normal to summon a guy in a suit from a bathroom stall at will. "He's my attorney." Max looked at Michael. "Where are we on the patent?"

Michael frowned, "Which one?"

"The Bob and Shush."

"Oh, it's nearly a done deal. Money should start rolling in within a few months."

Max looked at me with a smile on his face. "See?"

"How are you going to get them to pay you?" I asked.

"Good question. Michael?"

"Honor system? Paypal? I think they'll be grateful that their baby is quiet."

"So, it's donation-based?" I asked.

Michael cut in, "Yes, let's go with that. Okay, I gotta get back to it."

It was all too much for me. I didn't think the whole Bob and Shush thing was gonna work, but it wasn't my place to rain on Max's parade. He had pulled off a lot of miracles in the past. "Yeah, I'm leaving, too," I said.

"No, I'm going back to my office," Michael said, walking back into the stall. He closed the door behind him.

"Here's that smoothie, Aus," Max said, handing me a mug.

"How did you make it that quick?"

"This is a service business. We aim to please."

"Thanks," I said, grabbing the mug and tossing it back. "This is spectacular."

"You should incorporate green smoothies into your daily routine. You know how many antioxidants are in that?"

"Umm, a lot?" I asked.

"Dang straight there are."

THE BOOST from the green smoothie didn't last long. I had to figure out how to conserve energy or the Baby Bot could become an assassin and take me out. I spent most of math class listing the pros and cons of wearing a diaper permanently, so I didn't have to exert any effort walking to the bathroom. In the end, I decided my previous experience of wearing a diaper outside of Sophie's house during a love stakeout was too fresh and too wet to make it a permanent part of my wardrobe. Although the extra cushion could've been helpful in alleviating the bone bruises we got from sitting on the seemingly stone chairs at school.

I crumpled up my diaper papers and tossed them in the trash on the way out. I met Sophie down the hallway with a smile.

"Hey," I said, conjuring a cheerful attitude from the depths of my soul. "How is your day going?"

"Pretty good," Sophie said, smiling.

"Great. So, I was wondering, if maybe, you could take the

baby today? I think my spleen is shutting down. And my gall bladder is a mess." I grabbed my side with a wince for effect.

"I can't. I'm the President of the eighth grade. I'm a working mom. You have to pitch in, too."

"I have been! What am I supposed to do about my lymphatic system? It's definitely teetering on the edge."

"Your mind is teetering on the edge," Sophie said, shaking her head disapprovingly.

She was right. I was so tired that I walked straight into a wall. True, it was a moving wall, but a wall, nonetheless. I looked up at Mr. Muscalini, who looked down at me. "Did you see a fly around here? I thought I felt something on my chest."

"That was me, sir," I said.

"Not surprising," he said, and then furrowed his brow. "What's wrong, Davenport? You get duct taped to the school bus again?"

"You heard about that?" I asked. It was one of my most embarrassing moments. Flea had to tear me from the bus before it took off down the road. With my shirt. Leighton was really enthused about that one.

Mr. Muscalini continued, "Heard about it? It was in the teacher newsletter. It made my week."

"That hardly seems productive."

"So, what's eating at you, son?"

"I'm failing home ec and health."

"We are," Sophie added.

"Ahh, baby mania. It's tough." He slapped me on the shoulder, nearly shattering my collar bone. "Let me tell you what I know. Some men just aren't meant to be domesticated. Take me, for example. Many women have tried. They've seen my quads rippling in the summer sun. My eight pack of power."

"I thought it was nine?" I asked.

"It depends on where I'm at with my carbs. Anyway, they've seen my biceps, the size of boulders. And they try. But I'm just a wild stallion. I can't be tamed. It's not worth trying. You understand?"

"Not really, sir." I didn't understand Mr. Muscalini on most days when my brain power was at full capacity. There was no chance of comprehension at Baby Bot levels.

Mr. Muscalini didn't seem to care or realize. "Good. Glad to be of assistance. You know, Davenport. Even though you stink at sports, I kinda like you."

"I kinda like you too, sir."

"What do you think of my biceps?" Mr. Muscalini said, flexing.

"The best, sir."

"Good answer."

I HAD JUST GOTTEN the Baby Bot down to sleep. Its booming cries still echoed in my ears. I stared at the ceiling, not able to fall asleep, even though I was exhausted. I heard a quiet knock on the door.

My dad walked into my room, tentatively. "You awake?" he whispered.

"Yep," I said. "Unfortunately."

"Ain't that the truth," he said.

"Huh?"

"Nothing," he said, sitting down next to me. "I wanted to have a little talk with you."

"Alright," I said, not sure why he was being so weird. We talked all the time. I sat up and flipped on the light next to my bed.

My dad took a deep breath. "I was once your age and I know what you're going through."

I furrowed my brow. "Getting concussed via dodgeball? Stalked by a detention-obsessed principal?"

"No, not that, well, like... there are times...the thing about your age...you're growing up and things are changing."

Aaaahhh, farts. My temporarily-mediocre brain figured out what was going on. This wasn't just one of those regular talks. This was one of those important talks. The kind that both fathers and sons dread.

He continued, "So, you're changing. Like the seasons change. Winter. Spring. Summer. Fall. And you just need to go with the flow. Don't be afraid to ask questions."

"Can we be done with this?"

"Sure. That's about it, anyway. I think that went pretty well. So, you got it?"

"Absolutely," I lied. Not. I gave him a thumbs up and forced a smile, anyway.

"I feel good about this," my dad said, excitedly, seemingly proud of himself.

"Did you talk to Derek about this?" I asked. "I don't want him to miss out on such wisdom."

"Not yet, but great idea. I'm a little bit concerned he knows more than me."

"It wouldn't surprise me," I said.

I lay back down. The baby echo was gone. I just had to figure out how to forget all of the stuff I just heard.

15

I sat at the kitchen table, eating some scrambled eggs before school. My mother was cleaning up, as Derek entered with an "Aaaaahhhh, poo."

"What's wrong, babe?" my mother asked.

"My social life just cratered," he said, staring down at his pink t-shirt. "I'm an even bigger dork than Austin, as impossible as it seems."

I shook my head. "Thanks, a lot."

My mother huffed. "That's not nice, Derek."

"I speak the truth, woman. This stupid home economics class is ruining my life."

I actually agreed with him, for once.

Derek continued, "Every single clean shirt I have is pink!"

"I guess you learned not to mix a red shirt in with your whites," mom said.

"I have to wear this or dirty shirts.What can I do?"

"Oh, sorry. I can't help you. I'm not supposed to do your laundry for you."

"But I don't have any clean clothes," Derek whined.

"Yeah, you do. Right there," I said, pointing at his pink t-shirt.

"But it's pink."

"Then wear something dirty," I said.

"But that's gross. I'm just gonna go shirtless. Show off the pecks."

"You've been hanging around Mr. Muscalini too long," I said.

"You say that like it's a bad thing," Derek scoffed. "You want a ticket to the gun show?" Derek flexed his bicep.

"Hard pass," I said.

While we're on the subject of Mr. Muscalini and gym class, there was one good thing about the Baby Bots that I had noticed. The athletic kids were so tired from the Baby Bots being up all night, they could barely throw the dodgeballs.

In gym class that day, everything moved in slow motion.

Mike Jenkins, a pitcher on the baseball team, threw a ball directly at my head. Normally, I would've been knocked to the ground in like two seconds, but it came out of his hand so slow, I had time to fix my shirt, check the clock, and turn to the side to avoid the less-than-vicious attack. I yelled over to Ben, "This is awesome. I'm a dodgeball legend!"

And then my head exploded. I was dead. I lay on the ground, my soul readying to leave my body.

From another dimension, I heard Randy say, "I got a great night's sleep last night, Davenfart, because my baby is the best! I'm so refreshed."

I opened my eyes to see Randy standing over me. Out of the corner of his eye, he ripped a ball out of the air, and whizzed it at me, connecting with my solar plexus. I gasped for air and rolled to my side, as Randy laughed. The one time I wished Randy would've knocked me out with a dodgeball to the head so I could get some rest was, of course, the one time he didn't. I longed for the summer back at Camp Cherriwacka when I had a fabulous nap via dodge-ball concussion.

"I hate you," I whispered, curling up into a ball.

"I'm a father now, Davenfart. I don't have time for your immature and unevolved emotions."

"But you can still call me Davenfart?"

"That's your name, dude. Get some rest. You can't even remember your name."

After class was over, I limped to the locker room with Ben.

Ben asked, "Why is Randy so good at everything? How can he get his dumb baby to sleep when the rest of the eighth grade class is dying?"

"Maybe he knows the Bob and Shush? Or something better. I really think he's cheating somehow."

"How do you know?" Ben asked.

"Because he's always cheating."

"But he's also very good at everything."

"That's what's so annoying."

As we passed Mr. Muscalini's office, he called out, "Davenport!"

I entered his office. "Yes, sir."

"Derek is your brother, right?"

"Yes."

"You sure?"

I took a deep breath. "Yes. You've asked me that about twenty times over the past three years."

"Forgive me, but it is kind of unbelievable. I have a serious question for you," he asked. "Where did your brother get his butt chin from?"

"Unfortunately, it's natural." It was hardly a serious question, at least for a normal person.

"Dang it!" Mr. Muscalini nearly shattered his metal desk with his fist. "How can I be the best gym teacher ever without having the strongest chin around?"

"Is that the only thing you're missing, sir?" I asked, surprised. There was clearly more.

"You've seen me motivate this ragtag crew. How many butts have I whipped into shape around here? Nutrition plans churned out like a manufacturing plant? What if I try to glue it together with some sort of mold holding it in place?"

"I've tried that sir. There is no glue strong enough."

"What about duct tape?" he peppered.

"It did de-mustache Butt Hair on two occasions, but repositioning body parts is different than tearing off hair." I hadn't done any scientific experiments proving it, but I was pretty certain.

"What if I put it in some sort of retainer every night like you would do if you just got your braces off?" he asked.

"Those are just to hold it in shape after the braces do their job."

"Right. So, I need a full-time brace."

I asked, "What about a chin implant, sir?"

"This is all natural, son." Mr. Muscalini pointed to his biceps and then popped his pecks, mesmerized as they danced. "Look at 'em pop. Boogie woogie woogie." He looked up at me. "Where was I?"

"We were talking about chin implants."

"Oh, right. I draw the line there."

"What about makeup?" I asked, remembering my time with Maddie.

"I'm not the lipstick kinda guy, but do you think I could do some sort of shading technique? Do you know any Hollywood makeup artists or anything, Davenport?"

"Not currently, no."

"I'm horribly disappointed. My whole life has been a waste."

"Can I go now, sir? I'm gonna be late."

"I guess. But if your nerdiness comes up with anything, please let me know."

"Will do, sir," I said, hustling out of his office.

16

It was the big day. No, not Taco Tuesday. Not only was it Zorch's wedding day, but it was my social funeral as the oldest ring bearer in the history of marriage.

I stared at the oversized, wooden doors that led into the church, waiting for them to open, but hoping that they wouldn't.

Mr. Muscalini's voice whispered in my ear from behind me. "You nervous?"

I turned to look at him. "I wasn't until you just reminded me that I should be."

I was taken aback as I looked at him. He had a butt chin drawn on his face.

"Hey, what do you think of my chin? Notice anything different?" he asked, excitedly.

I didn't know what to say. I thought as quickly as I could.

He continued without my answer. "I hired the school's best artist, Emmy Henry."

I forced a smile. "Sir, it looks spectacular. You could crash the Davenport family reunion and no one would be the wiser."

"I don't know what that means, but I'm taking it as a positive," he said, smiling. "You nervous?" he asked, again.

"I forgot I was supposed to be."

Mr. Muscalini crouched down. "Here's what we're gonna do. It's a simple Go route like in football."

I stared at him, not understanding anything. To me, the words simple and football just didn't belong together. "You'll have to be more specific, sir."

"Haven't I taught you anything over the last three years, Davenport?"

Not a whole lot, I thought. "Of course, but I just don't get football routes. Except for the 44 Blast. Love that one."

"Oh, baby. That one is spectacular. I remember one time when your brother-"

"Sir?" I didn't really need to hear a highlight from my brother's football career. "What's your advice?"

"Take a deep breath and when you see an opening, fill the gap, and go. Straight up to the alter as fast as you can."

"But they told me to take long, slow steps," I said.

"Those are the people who get crushed in the backfield. You gotta keep your steps short and quick, so you can cut in traffic."

"Got it." I did not. At all. Was I going to be tackled? Was the ring the ball? Who knew when Mr. Muscalini was involved?

"Alright. I'm headin' out there," Mr. Muscalini said. "Chin held high. Get it?"

"Yes," I said, smiling. But I wish I hadn't.

Mr. Muscalini scooted off to a side door and disappeared, leaving me and the Maid of Honor. I heard the music start inside the church. I knew it was only a matter of time. But the longer I waited, the more nervous I got. I still wasn't sure if Mr. Muscalini would have Nick DeRozan waiting to crush me or not.

But when the doors opened, it wasn't as daunting a task as I feared. I quickly found Sophie and locked eyes with her, just putting one foot in front of the other. The rest of my crew was there with her, all smiling at me. I heard a few chuckles. I didn't look to see who it was, but I knew it was Randy and his group of evil doers. I didn't really care. Nobody had tackled me. Yet.

I did get some heckling, though. I heard someone chuckle and say, "Nice tails, mermaid."

I looked around the room. Cheeks was there, looking miserable, as usual. Mrs. Funderbunk stood in front of a trio of orchestra string players, conducting. I was halfway to the alter where Zorch, Mr. Muscalini, and his new butt chin were waiting for me with smiles.

And then the apocalypse began. A baby started crying behind me. And then another. And another. I glanced over to see Amanda Gluskin fussing with her Baby Bot in the crowd. Why the heck did anyone invite her?

Mrs. Funderbunk turned around while still directing the musicians. "Shush!"

Amanda Gluskin's head jerked up from her Baby Bot. "You can't shush my baby!"

The musicians still played, but by the looks on their faces, weren't quite sure if they should continue.

Mrs. Funderbunk turned around again, her face boiling. She also seemingly amped up the tempo of the musicians, probably due to her rising blood pressure. They were playing at three times the normal rate. She yelled, "I can and I will shush you, too!"

Due to the increased tempo, I quickened my own pace down the aisle. I was almost there.

"I dare you!" Amanda yelled back, as we all just stared at them.

"I dare you!"

I wasn't even sure what was going on, but I was pretty certain that Amanda would have Mrs. Funderbunk in a Camel Clutch before the bride even entered, which would be another wedding record.

And then an even bigger commotion ensued. Of course, it was me in the middle of it, hurdling through the air. I was kind of bored of commotions. They were like a weekly event for me.

Due to my rapid pace and Randy's oversized foot somehow being thrust into the aisle just as I made my way past, I took flight, falling forward. I held onto the pillow for dear life, but unfortunately the wedding rings were not secured to it. They also took flight. A lot more flight than I did, soaring into the air.

The music stopped playing. The crowd chatter fell to a hush. Well, besides the laughter coming from Randy and his friends. I didn't really care. I was most concerned with not smashing my face on the floor, but also modestly concerned with not losing the rings, so I glanced up to try to find them.

Much to my surprise (and everyone else's), out of the corner of my eye, I saw Ms. Armpit Hair do a front flip out of the front pew from a standstill, landing perfectly on the other side. In high heels, no less. She stood up and thrust her hands in the air, just as the two rings descended toward her.

I crashed to the ground with a thud and a grunt, and then looked up. Ms. Armpit Hair steadied her outstretched fingers beneath the rings, lining them up beneath the rings' paths. The rings encircled Ms. Armpit Hair's fingers perfectly. The crowd exploded into cheers. Zorch and Mr. Muscalini hugged. Mr. Muscalini squeezed Zorch so hard that I thought his head might pop.

I stood up and dusted myself off, thankful I didn't lose the rings. Three-year old ring bearers had done a better job than I did. Like all of them. I straightened my mermaid tails and walked over to Ms. Pierre, as Randy and crew heckled me.

"Nice catch," I said, as Zorch and Mr. Muscalini surrounded her.

"Thank you," Ms. Pierre said, handing me the bride's ring.

I placed the ring on my fluffy pillow, longing to switch places with the ring, and lay my sweet head down for a long nap. It took me a bit to return to the moment to realize there was trouble. A lot of it.

Ms. Pierre tugged at Zorch's ring that was on her ring finger, to no avail. "It's stuck," she said, with a grunt.

"What are we gonna do?" I asked.

Zorch looked like he was gonna puke. At least he wouldn't have to be the one to clean it up for once.

Mr. Muscalini said confidently, "Let me see, Ms. Arm, errr...Pierre." He tugged at it. "Why don't we just tear it off?"

"She tried that. The ring won't come off," Zorch said, wiping the sweat off his brow.

"I meant her finger."

The reverend interjected, "We'd like for the guests to keep all limbs and appendages."

"At least before the main course," Zorch said, attempting to add some humor to a less-than-funny situation. I wasn't so sure about that. With Miss Geller's cooking, she might want to make finger sandwiches. I'm not a cannibal or anything, but I wasn't convinced that would be the worst thing on the menu.

Mrs. Funderbunk walked over and said, "The show must go on!"

Somebody called out from the crowd, "This isn't Broadway. It's a wedding."

Zorch nodded to Cheeks. He stood up and walked over to us.

Zorch looked at Cheeks and said, "We have to put our custodial minds together. We've been in jams bigger than this."

"I'll just rip it off," Mr. Muscalini said, as if he hadn't brought it up before.

"We don't need anyone losing any appendages today," Zorch said. He looked at Cheeks again. "Remember when Scotty Lipton's foot went on fire, so he put it in the toilet and it got stuck?"

Mr. Muscalini chimed in. "I thought he lost his foot."

"Okay, forget about that one," Zorch said, quickly. "Remember when Suzie Aikman got her braces stuck to the water fountain?"

Cheeks said, "She was stuck for like four hours."

"Okay. Bad example. My brain isn't working," Zorch said.

As embarrassing as it was to bring it up, I had an idea. "I had a umm, friend, one time that got caught in a doggie door. They used butter."

"Who has butter in a church?" Cheeks asked.

"Good point," I said.

Ms. Armpit Hair said, "What about the holy water?"

"You will not," the reverend said.

"That's fair," Zorch said.

Cheeks said, "Okay, I'll do it."

"Do what?" we all asked in unison.

"Suck on her finger."

Ms. Pierre's face morphed ghost.

"Just don't pull it! She might fart!" Someone yelled from the crowd.

Ernie Stroman came forward with a bunch of brown goop in his hands. "Here, try this," he said.

"What is that?" Zorch asked. I thought he would've known being that the stuff had been sprayed all over the school, wiped on lockers, pranked into sandwiches, among other things.

Ernie shrugged. "It's like pudding."

"It's like pudding?" Mr. Muscalini said. "What's the sugar content?"

"Smell it. It's not bad."

Ms. Armpit Hair leaned down and smelled Ernie's pie of Baby Bot poo. She shrugged. "I smell a hint of thyme in there."

"Who puts thyme in pudding?" Mr. Muscalini said.

"That's not the point," I said. "Just do it."

Ernie rubbed the Baby Bot poo on our esteemed principal. Most of the students in the crowd chuckled. Ms. Pierre turned the ring, the poo seeping between the ring and her skin.

Mr. Muscalini put his hands on the ring and pulled. He nearly tumbled over, but he held onto the ring, and Ms. Pierre didn't fart, which was a bonus.

Mr. Muscalini handed me the poopy ring and said, "I know you and your carb intake. Don't even think about eating this pudding. Go rinse it off before the bride gets here."

"Thanks for the heads up," I said. "I was looking forward to licking it clean."

Zorch chuckled. Mr. Muscalini didn't realize I was joking and looked disgusted.

"What was that?" Zorch asked me, privately.

"Baby Bot poo," I said. It was the first positive to come out of the Baby Bot, both literally and figuratively.

"Lovely," Zorch said.

SURPRISINGLY, the rest of the ceremony went off without a hitch. Well, they did get hitched, and with no other issues. I stood with my crew at the cocktail hour, staring at my plate in disbelief. The appetizers were horrid. I was kicking myself for not warning the Center for Disease Control. I did learn something important, though. A myth had been busted. Not everything tastes great wrapped in bacon. I thought it was the only thing that would work, but the problem was not the bacon. It was the booger-like substance inside.

Thankfully, my attention was drawn to Mr. Muscalini nearly shattering a glass as he clanked his fork against it with the force of a lumberjack.

Mr. Muscalini cleared his throat and adjusted his jacket. It was a risk to mess with it. The tux was so tight, it looked like the thing could blow from the slightest of movements. "Can I have your attention, please? This is a very special evening," he said, beaming at the bride and groom. "The union of marriage is a most cherished coupling, like a doubles tennis partnership. You have to work together when life is whizzing at your head at a hundred miles an hour. I would also say it's like a pitcher and catcher relationship. Life may throw you a curveball..."

Zorch gave Mr. Muscalini the 'get on with it' look or maybe it was the 'knock off the sports references' look. I wasn't too sure.

Mr. Muscalini continued, "Right. Umm, let's get to the good stuff. May the sun shine upon your marriage like it does on my bulging, glistening biceps." He looked at the crowd. "You know how hard it was to find a tuxedo jacket that fit these bad boys? They had this shipped from Greenland from some lumberjack town."

Zorch shot Mr. Muscalini another look.

"Where was I? Oh yeah, may you stay the course when you're met with rocky waters like my rippling quads that look like a category-five white-water-rafting adventure. They really are a thing of beauty, just like our bride." He smiled at the now Mrs. Zorch and continued, "And that reminds me. May all your stomachs be as strong as my kevlar abs as we sit down to eat the Curious Chicken. If you believe in a higher power, now is the time to call in the favors."

Zorch's eyes nearly bulged out of his head, while a few teachers and students stifled laughs. Mrs. Zorch's face reddened.

Mr. Muscalini raised his champagne glass. "And now, we toast. To the bride and groom. And my abs. All nine of them." I guess Mr. Muscalini had tightened up his carb intake since our last conversation.

There was a smattering of applause, some confusion, and a lot of relief that the speech was over.

Without warning, Mr. Muscalini blew his whistle into the microphone, nearly killing all the dogs within a one-mile radius of the wedding hall. "Let's get this party started on the dance floor. Move table number five. Move. Move. Move! Let's go, Granny! Shake it! Woah, not that much. You're gonna bust a hip or something."

The D.J./M.C. rushed over to Mr. Muscalini and tried to grab the mic out of his hand, but Mr. Muscalini instinctively threw a stiff arm, blasting the poor man to the floor. The crowd gasped.

Mr. Muscalini stared at everyone. "What are you all looking at?" He looked at Granny again. "Move it or lose it, sister!"

And then Zorch and Mrs. Zorch caught Mr. Muscalini's eye. They started slow dancing in the center of the floor, her head on his shoulder. Mr. Muscalini melted and handed the mic over to the relieved M.C., who was still catching his breath.

As I was heading to my table, I saw Mr. Muscalini off to the side of the wedding hall. He was staring at the wall and seemingly wiping his eyes a lot. I walked over to him, curious.

"Mr. Muscalini? Are you okay?" I asked, tentatively.

He turned to me, his eyes wet and puffy.

"Of course," Mr. Muscalini said, defensively. "I'm sweating from my eyes." But then he burst out, crying. "Isn't this beautiful?"

"The wall, sir?" I asked, confused.

"The wedding, Davenport." Mr. Muscalini put his hulking hands on my shoulders. "Promise me something, Davenport."

"Yes, sir?"

"You love. Love without limit. Without fear of rejection. I don't care that your muscles are like teeny, tiny bumps. Little pimples on an old lady's butt..."

"Is there a point to this?" I asked, not overly enthused with the direction we were going.

"Yes. I'm getting there." Mr. Muscalini pulled a handkerchief out of his suit pocket and blew his nose harder than a rocket launch at Cape Canaveral.

I wiped the spray from my face, so very eager to hear

what he wanted to tell me.

Finally, he continued, "You've got one huge muscle. And it's the most important one."

"My brain?" I said, unsure.

"No, dummy. Your heart. Keep flexing it. Don't...ever...stop." He held in tears, and said between sniffles, "Excuse me." Mr. Muscalini ran off, nearly knocking Zorch's grandma over.

I made my way over to the table where all my friends were already seated. I slipped into my seat in between Sophie and Ben.

"Everything okay?" Sophie asked.

"Mr. Muscalini," was all I could say.

"Gotcha," Sophie said, holding in a laugh.

A waiter, who seemed barely older than me, came over to our table. He smiled and said, "Good evening. My name is Phillip. I will be your server. Any food allergies at the table?"

I looked around at my crew. Everyone shook their heads, no.

"Okay, good. No allergies. Our main course tonight is meatloaf."

We all looked at each other. Mrs. Geller-Zorch's meatloaf was barely more edible than poison.

I threw my hand up. "Did you say allergies? I am actually allergic to meatloaf."

"Me, too!" Sophie said.

Ben chimed in. "Since there are multiple meatloaf allergies at the table, we should all probably pass. What else is there?"

"Very good. Well, we have Tofurkey loaf with peppermint and French onion soup."

Cheryl raised her hand. "I'm allergic to Tofurkey loaf with peppermint."

"So the French onion?" Phillip suggested.

"Probably tastes like French bunion," I whispered to Sophie. I looked up at the waiter. "Is there bread for the soup?"

"Yes, of course."

"I'll take a loaf," I said, as confidently as I could.

Phillip frowned. "A loaf? That's not possible."

"I'm the ring bearer. Make it possible."

"Yes, sir," Phillip said.

"Make that two!" Ben added.

We were betting that Mrs. Geller-Zorch did not bake the bread, and on the off chance that she did, it was really hard to screw up bread to the point that it would make us puke.

Without warning, I was hit in the back of the head with something. It didn't really hurt, but I said, "Oww," like a tough guy, anyway. I turned around to see a handful of masked kids decorating the wedding hall with toilet paper. Streams of it were flying everywhere. It was dark, but I could tell one of them was Randy. I stood up, wanting to rip the mask off Randy as he ran by to, well, unmask him and catch him in the midst of a most heinous act.

I didn't predict that, as he ran toward me, he would unleash another roll of toilet paper directly at my head. I ducked, but it was too late. He had the advantage and was only two steps away from me by the time I turned back toward him. He threw out an elbow, catching me in the shoulder. I stumbled back, tripped over Sophie, who was behind me, and hit my head on the table with a crash.

"Are you okay?" Sophie asked, before I even hit the floor.

I hit the floor with a thud. "Sorry for the delay. I was waiting for all the data to be in. The answer is a resounding no."

Ben, Luke, and Just Charles took me to the bathroom. As

bad as it was, having three escorts was a bit much. My ears rang, as Ben pushed the door open. I immediately felt an improvement. Standing before us was none other than my favorite bathroom attendant, Max Mulvihill.

"Aus the Boss! I was hoping you would come visit," Max said with a smile.

"Max? What are you doing here?" I managed to say.

Max shook his head, laughing. "Who else did you think would be here?" Max finally noticed the guys holding me up. "What's wrong? What happened?"

"Got run over. Again," I said, softly.

"Warblemacher?" Max asked.

"The one and only," Ben said.

"Okay. Well, we're gonna have to run some tests. Ben, grab an ice pack from the freezer under the sink."

"Freezer under the sink?" Ben asked, as he headed over.

Max stepped in front of me. "Follow my finger with your eyes."

He moved his finger up and down, side to side. I did my best to follow.

"Good," Max said. "Do you feel nauseous?"

"No."

"That's surprising with meatloaf on the menu," Max said, impressed. "You must have an iron stomach."

"No, I just ordered the bread. I invoked my ring bearer privileges."

Max stood up and walked over to the wall. He grabbed a ring that was attached to a string and pulled. An oversized eye chart appeared on the wall out of nowhere.

"What the-" Just Charles said under his breath.

Max said, "Read line four for me starting with the G."

"I normally can't read from this far away. And where did you get that?" I asked, curiously.

"I'm asking the questions, Aus. Head injuries are no joking matter. If only I had my CT machine, I could do a CAT scan, but it's in the shop. Very temperamental."

"Well, when you're dealing with the heads of kids in my school, I understand that," I said.

"No slurred speech. Do you have any memory loss?" Max asked.

"You mean, do I remember forgetting anything?" I asked, chuckling. "I don't think so."

"Ringing ears? Disorientation?"

"My ears rang, but I'm feeling okay now," I said.

Max stood up. "I don't think you have a concussion, but if you do get any of the symptoms I mentioned, see Nurse Nova immediately."

Luke whispered to Ben, "Who is this guy?"

"It's Max Mulvihill. He's the Harry Potter of bathroom attendants."

"Can he teach me to dance?"

"I didn't say he was Seamus Finnegan. I said he was Harry Potter," Ben said, chuckling.

"So, that's a yes?" Luke asked.

Max chimed in, "I heard something about dancing. Fast or slow? I've got video viewing booths set up in stalls 4-6. Just swipe a credit card and choose your style."

"Credit card?" Luke asked.

"I'll take cash, but I don't do receipts. I run a paperless organization."

My eyes bulged. "Even in there?" I asked, pointing to the stall. "You know, for everything?"

"No, not in there. But I even sold a bunch of toilet paper to Warblemacher before. 60% markup. Fool should get it delivered from Amazon on subscription."

I wasn't convinced that Randy was a typical TP

purchaser, but it was great to finally get some evidence on him.

17

I zombied my way through the next day, barely making it. I was grateful that Sophie had the Demon Bot for the night. I sat at the dinner table with Derek and my parents. We had grilled cheese and tomato soup. It wasn't the typical meal in my house, but my mom had been craving it. I didn't mind the grilled cheese, but I was so tired, I thought that I might drown in my soup. I was thankful that my parents were there to save me if I fell in. That's just one more reason I hated the Baby Bot and its creators. One would think they would give a warning to us kids. Don't eat soup when the lifeguard isn't on duty or there is no parental supervision.

My brother was unusually quiet, which I enjoyed.

"This is the strangest dinner I've ever been at with these two, maybe ever," my dad said. "You guys are moving slower than molasses." He laughed.

My mother joined in. "Normally, they don't even use spoons. They just slurp their soups down, Medieval Times style."

"Very funny," I said, taking a bite of my grilled cheese.

Derek put down his spoon and looked at my parents. "I have a serious question."

"What is it?" my mother asked, her face dropping. Derek didn't normally ask serious questions.

"Do they have Baby Bots at LaSalle Military School?"

"I don't think so," my mother answered, confused.

Derek's face brightened. "Can I finish out the school year there?"

What was happening? Were my dreams coming true? Would my life finally have meaning? My heart pounded. I crossed my fingers and held my breath that they would say yes.

Derek continued, "I can't take it."

He needed a break from his weeks-old baby. I needed a break from my 13-year old brother.

My father interjected, "No. You can't quit at the first sign of struggle."

"I'm literally going to die. My spleen is shutting down. I can feel it. Austin, back me up here."

I took a deep breath and hammed it up. "It pains me to say it," I said, lying. "I think he should go. Spleens are shutting down all across Cherry Avenue. There's a line out the nurse's door," I said, hoping to help Derek's cause. And my own.

"You think military school will be easy?" my dad asked.

"No, but it will be different. As long as I don't have to change diapers and I get a full-night sleep. I can handle the rest."

"It's not happening," my mother said.

"Sorry, dude," my dad added.

"But, Dad!"

It was an odd discussion, to say the least. My parents were always threatening to send Derek to LaSalle. Now, he wanted to go and they wouldn't let him. Parents...you try to raise 'em right, but sometimes you have to give them some responsibility and let them crash and burn.

I HUSTLED from science class to Cherry Avenue, arriving before Advisory, so I had a few minutes with my friends. It was a doozy. Cheryl walked up to Charles with the stroller and said in front of everyone, "Charles, it's over."

Charles furrowed his brow. "What's over?"

"Us."

"What? Why?" he asked, confused. Tears welled up in his eyes.

"You're not committed to us," Cheryl said, simply.

"Who's us?"

Cheryl shook her head. "See? You don't even know. Me and the baby."

"Are you serious? It's a rubber doll that we're going to give back in a few weeks."

"That doesn't matter." Cheryl took a deep breath. "Good bye, Charles." She turned the stroller and walked away. Sophie and Sammie followed her.

Just Charles ran after Cheryl, and returned a minute later. I put my hand on his shoulder.

He was holding in tears. "I can't...believe Cheryl...broke up...with....me."

"You guys were dating? I thought she was your cousin or something," Randy said, walking by with a smirk.

"Shut your mouth, Warblemacher," I said.

Randy just laughed and kept going.

"What are you gonna do about Chip?" I asked, not sure why I cared about the stupid Baby Bot.

"She agreed to joint custody. I get Monday and Thursday, and every other weekend."

"Oh, man. This is bad."

Just Charles shook his head, staring down at the ground. "Everything was great until we had kids. Chip drained the life out of our relationship. When the fun died, the love died."

Life was getting way too complicated. "I feel like this should be an after-school TV special. Or maybe reality TV," I said.

"What am I gonna do? I can't raise a baby alone."

I had to end the nonsense. "Dude, it's just plastic."

"Oh, yeah. Forgot about that. But still, what am I gonna do without Cheryl? I miss her already. I think I'm gonna hurl."

"Well, that could just be the cafeteria food," Ben said, joining the conversation. "Kelly Flynn puked on the bus. It splattered everywhere. It looked like yesterday's scary steak sandwich."

"Not helping, Benjamin," I said.

"Oh, sorry," Ben said, shrugging.

I walked Just Charles to Advisory. "Don't worry, man. I've been through this. It'll get better."

It did not get better. As soon as we finished the Pledge of Allegiance, the Speaker of Doom crackled. Ms. Armpit Hair said, "Good morning, Gophers. It's been such a difficult time for our eight graders managing their new robotic offspring that we thought we would make something fun out of it. Next Friday night, Cherry Avenue Middle School will host the first-ever Baby Bonanza! We will take everything that you've learned in your home economics and health class and turn it into a contest. Also, if your friends and family would like to attend, it will cost $5. That money will be used to purchase a statue of me for the Gopher Garden. Have a great day!"

Groans rang out like a chorus of five hundred angry whales. We were all so tired, it came out in slow motion.

"Aaahhh, farts," I said, hanging my head in my hands. A contest to show off our baby-nurturing abilities. Things were just peachy at Cherry Avenue Middle School.

I STOOD with Ben in the gym locker room, readying for one of Mr. Muscalini's life lessons that typically risk my life.

"I hate this," Ben said.

"I know. My Baby Bot's whole life is eat, poop, sleep," I said.

Randy nearly hurled a few lockers down. "Your baby eats poop? That's gross, dude. But I guess it's not unexpected given that your name is Davenfart."

"Funny, Randy. I wish you would've puked. It would've been the best thing that ever came out of your mouth," I countered.

"You excited to get crushed in the Baby Bonanza, Davenfart? I'm gonna squash you and your wittle baby. What's his name, anyway? Davenfart Junior?"

"You think I care if you're better at me at changing diapers?" I asked, chuckling.

"You apparently don't care that I'm better at you at everything. That's why you always get crushed," Randy said, shutting his locker. Thankfully, he disappeared, heading out toward class.

I stood in front of my locker, getting ready for gym class. I kept zoning in and out.

Ben shook my shoulder. "Dude! Wake up! We're gonna

be late for class."

"Just leave me, man," I said, wobbling back and forth.

"You don't have the energy to run laps for being late. Muscalini is gonna lose his marbles if you don't get your thirty-seven minutes of physical activity for the day."

"Just go, dude. Save yourself," I groaned.

"You're not dying, dude," Ben said, shutting his locker.

"I might be. My pancreas is shutting down. I can feel it."

"Knock it off and hurry up. You gotta get dressed. I'm not waiting for you. I'm not running laps for being late."

"Toodles, Benjamin."

I nodded off for a minute. Or ten. I had no idea how long I was leaning against the cool metal locker. And I heard Mr. Muscalini yelling in the distance. At first, I thought he was in my dreams. Scary thought, I know. Thankfully, it was real life, but that meant that I was late for class.

I ran to the door in super slow motion, Hollywood-style. I'm sure it looked awesome. You know what didn't look awesome? My wardrobe as I entered the gym, which was filled to the brim with my classmates, both boys and girls. What was the problem with my wardrobe you ask? I was missing a key item. At first, I didn't realize what the problem was. Everybody was pointing at me and laughing, which was not uncommon on most days, but then I heard Randy say, "Davenfart's got no pants on!"

I looked down to see nothing but my bare, stick-figure legs and sneakers. It wasn't the first time the school saw me in my underwear, but that experience didn't help much. Perhaps, you remember my wardrobe malfunction during the Santukkah! school play? This was on par with that.

Mr. Muscalini cocked his head and said, "Hey, Davenport?"

"Yes, sir?"

"Sky's out, thighs out? I like it! But you might want to bulk those twigs up a bit."

"Twiggy Davenfart. I like it," Randy called out. "Or should we call you Pinky?"

I looked down to see my previously tighty whiteys were actually tighty pinkies. The Baby Bot just kept getting better and better.

"Alright, let's get started," Mr. Muscalini boomed.

I walked with Ben and Ian Kuster out to the track.

"I can't believe I did that," I said. "Sophie's gonna kill me."

"Don't worry, dude," Ben said. "I was so tired, I gave a bottle to my dog. I think he liked it."

"You don't even have a dog, Ben," I said, frowning.

"Holy smokes! You're right. I was sitting outside on the deck. I wonder what I was feeding? It did kinda smell like a skunk."

Ian Kuster added, "I'm wearing two different shoes."

"At least you're wearing underwear," I said.

"Am I? How do you know?" Ian said. He checked in his shorts and let out a sigh of relief. "Yep. Golden." At least they weren't pink.

"We gotta figure this Baby Bot out. It's ruining our lives. Just Charles got dumped. I'm walking around school in my underwear. Ben's feeding coyotes. This has to stop," I said, pounding my fist into my hand. "Oww," I said.

"Let's science the heck out of this," Ben said.

"I don't have time for this. I have to do real science work. First midterm of my high school career. My college records are at stake. MIT could be out the window because of the stupid Baby Bot 2000."

～

BEN and I lay on opposite couches in my den, enjoying the quiet. Both our Baby Bots were with the girls. My head pounded worse than it did from any beating Derek ever gave me. Possibly more than all of Derek's beatings combined. It was that bad. If my brain was working to its normal supreme capacity, I would ponder how humans have survived all these years. If fake parenting is this hard, how hard is real parenting? I was in survival mode. All options were on the table.

"Dude, I can't take this anymore. We have to do something," I groaned.

"What can we do?" Ben asked.

"Hire a nanny?"

"Yes. Let's do that."

I called out to the kitchen. "Dad, how much does a nanny cost?"

"Dude, not so loud. My head hurts," Ben said, rubbing his temples.

"Umm, a guy at work pays his nanny $600 a week."

"$600 a week?" Ben yelped.

"Dude, not so loud," I said. "My head hurts, too. How are we gonna get $600? I don't even think I can manage $6 a week."

"That's a start, bro," Ben said, excitedly.

"That's like a twenty minute break," I said, my brain still capable of something, at least.

"Let's do it," Ben said. "No, I got it! We can start a babysitting ring. $15 an hour. We each do twenty hours and see if the nanny will watch both babies."

"Umm, why would we do that? We're gonna babysit lots of real babies so we can pay someone to watch two fake ones?" I asked.

"Yeah, that was a bad idea. Can't we just put on the

Disney channel and be done with this? That's how my parents raised me and I turned out okay."

"That's debatable," I said, chuckling.

"Very funny," Ben said.

"I thought so."

By THE TIME the next morning rolled around, we still didn't have any solutions. As bad as it was, the nanny idea was still at the top of our list. But the economics were still way off. And I had bigger issues to deal with, at least for the moment. I had my first big high school test, a science midterm. If I wasn't so tired, I would be freaking out. Unfortunately, given my Baby Bot problem, I hadn't studied much. I kept falling asleep on my books, drooling all over the place.

I sat next to Flea in science class, about to take the midterm. I tried to figure out if I could use my extra pencil to prop an eye open or something, but I couldn't get the ergonomics right. How many middle school/high school kids have both economic and ergonomic problems? It just wasn't fair. I stared down at the test before me. It could've been French for all I knew. I could barely make out the words, let alone do anything complex.

What made things worse is that I didn't even have the chance to try. I jolted awake to the end-of-period bell. I looked around the room, not sure what the heck was going on.

Miss Kelvin said, "I'm sure everyone did wonderfully. Just hand in your test on the way out."

The rest of my class packed up and began to head out. I

nearly pulled my hair out, as I stared at the test on the desk in front of me.

"I can't believe this," I said, shocked. "I'm gonna fail. Me. I'm gonna fail."

Flea looked over and said, "I'm sure it's not that bad."

"I didn't even finish. I barely started. I answered more questions with drool than actually answers."

Flea looked over at my test, his brow furrowed. "Hey, but that drool circles the right answer there and there," he said, pointing to two questions on the test.

I was less than enthused.

"Wait a second. Oh. My. God. Who cares what you get on this? You're gonna be rich!"

"What? What are you talking about?" I asked, confused.

Flea pointed to my exam. "That drool looks like Lady Gaga. You could get an A in art for that. Or sell it on eBay. I'd pay ten bucks for that."

"Thanks for your support, Flea," I said, not really thankful at all.

I grabbed my test and slipped out of my seat. In that very moment, I declared a flat-out war against the Baby Bot 2000. I had had enough. Even Derek and Randy, on their worst days, had never pushed me this far. My life was crumbling. I had to do something. But first, I needed to salvage the test.

I walked up to Miss Kelvin and said, "I don't know if you know this or not, but in eighth grade, we have these pretend babies that are really annoying and keep us up all night, and I was so exhausted I fell asleep during the test."

"Oh, that's not good. Do you want me to whip up a natural sleep remedy for the baby?"

"No, it's plastic. I'd like to retake the test, if possible."

She grabbed the test from me and looked it over. "Let me see here. Oh, that drool looks like a strand of DNA. I can give you extra credit for that." She pointed to a booger on page two. "That snot is a little wet, but I'd say it's still solid matter, which is the answer to that question. You're looking pretty good."

"What do you think I'll get?"

"Right now, I'm thinking you're at least in double digits."

"Double digits?" I asked, nearly throwing up in my mouth. "I've never gotten below an A in science my entire life."

"Well, there's a first time for everything." Miss Kelvin continued to scan the test. "You've got a twelve, at least."

"A twelve?" My voice rose four octaves.

"At least," she said, confidently.

"This is a disaster. I'll never get into M.I.T. with this."

"Oh, absolutely not."

Ahhhh, farts.

∽

I CALLED AN EMERGENCY MEETING. Just the boys. The girls were way too attached to the Baby Bots. They couldn't be included in our plans to take them down. I sat with Ben, Luke, and Just Charles in my basement, chomping on some pretzels.

"We need to science the heck out of these things," I said.

"That was my idea," Ben said.

"I know. It was a good one," I said. "And quite humorous, as I'm failing science at the moment."

"But how?" Just Charles asked. "I've been keeping journals and I've found no discernible patterns. I've even run the data through an AI program. Nothing."

"What if we hack the baby?" I asked.

"To pieces?" Ben yelled in shock.

"No! Like computer hack. It's not a real baby, remember?"

"Don't tell Sammie that. She likes it better than me," Ben said, disappointed.

"Yeah, we all do, but that's not the point. It's run by software. Let's hack it."

"Maybe we can control it by our computer rather than by having to feed it," Luke said.

Just Charles added, "Maybe we can write a program that makes it think we're doing all those dumb things that babies need without doing any of them. Do you think they have a security system or something?"

"Who would hack a baby?" I asked. "I mean that's ridiculous. Where do you think the computer is?"

Ben ran his fingers through his hair. "Please don't be in his butt. Please don't be in his butt."

I shrugged. "Let's find out."

We undressed the Baby Bot and turned it over onto his stomach. We all leaned in for a better look. Footsteps creaked down the stairs, as we examined the butt.

"Why are you staring at the baby's butt?" Derek asked.

"We, well, umm, just wanted to make sure it was clean," I said.

Derek shrugged, grabbed a hockey stick, and headed back upstairs. "You guys are so weird."

Once Derek was out of ear shot, I muttered, "Where is the computer?" I took a closer look. "This isn't good."

"What?" Ben asked.

"Look at the crease on the hips, from his waist to his thigh," I said, pointing.

"Oh, no," Just Charles said.

"Yep. You have to pop open the baby's butt," I said.

"I'm not touching the baby's butt," Just Charles said.

"You've cleaned it. Why can't you touch it?" I asked.

Ben added, "It's not real. It's rubber."

"Then *you* touch it. It's your baby," Just Charles said, defensively.

"Yeah, just put your fingers in the crack and pry it open," Luke added.

"That just sounds gross." I did as I was instructed. "I should've worn my..." And then things went awry. The baby's bottom vibrated like a 6.2 earthquake and blasted a geyser of brown goo directly into my face. Sheepishly, I continued, "Goggles."

Everyone cracked up, no pun intended. Ben handed me a clean diaper and said, "For your butt face." Everyone cracked up even more.

I just shook my head, as I wiped the goo from my brow. I rinsed off in the sink and returned to the Baby Bot. I wasn't going to give up that easily.

"Where does it keep all that stuff?" Ben asked, refusing to get too close.

"Are both his legs filled with poo?" Luke asked.

"I read on Twitter that it has some sort of expanding compound. When the water mixes with the formula powder inside the stomach, it starts to grow," I said.

"So, we should stop feeding it?" Luke asked.

"Yeah. That'll work," I said, chuckling.

Just Charles took over where I left off. I guess he was gambling that the little bundle of poo was fresh out. He yelled, "That's it!"

"We've found it?" Ben said, as if he had done something to actually help.

"What did you find? Its irritable bowel?" I asked.

Just Charles said, "That thing is beyond irritable. It's downright irate." He looked up inside the doll to see a case and wires. "Here goes nothing." He slid his hand in and gripped the case.

"You're okay doing that, but you couldn't crack its crack?" I asked.

He ignored me. "I'm going to pick the baby up. The case is stuck. Maybe gravity will help. Plus, your fingers are smaller."

I did as I was told. Just Charles held the Baby Bot up in the air, the Baby Bot butt in my face. I reached up and grabbed the case. I couldn't get a good grip on the plastic. My face was right in front of its butt, which was a bit scary, given my recent history. My fingers slipped. I squeezed harder. I heard something beep. And then the baby snapped. Like mental breakdown snap. The Baby Bot's arms started pumping up and down, pummeling Just Charles in the face. Its legs raced like it was in the Olympics, stomping on my face, inflicting blows so severe, I thought I might not survive.

Just Charles tossed the baby in the air before crumpling to the ground with a thud. Ben, instinctively reached out and grabbed the baby. It proceeded to karate chop Luke to the temple and kick Ben in the throat. That's all I remember before darkness fell upon me.

I woke up with my father, brother, and friends staring at me, as I lay flat on my back on the basement floor.

My dad raised an eyebrow and asked, "Are you okay?"

"That was the best sleep I've had since the demon baby arrived," I whispered. "But my face hurts."

"It hurts us, too." Derek shook his head. "You got knocked out by a plastic doll? You've hit a new low. I'm truly ashamed."

"I'm refreshed," I said, getting up.

"Drink some lemonade and you can be refreshed without losing your dignity, dork."

"Knock it off, Derek," my dad said.

"Thanks for the advice," I said to Derek.

"So, this plastic doll knocked all four of you unconscious?" my dad asked, scratching his head. "You guys are in worse shape than I thought."

"The thing hit me in the temple! I think it's programmed for like Brazilian Ju-Jitsu or something," Luke said, defensively.

"I think my larynx is crushed," Ben said, softly.

"You guys are all being a little dramatic, don't you think?' my dad asked.

Derek shook his head and went back upstairs.

"Anybody need medical attention?"

We all shook our heads, no. Emotional support? Definitely.

18

I sat at the kitchen table, doing homework after dinner. My mother walked in, a concerned look on her face.

"What's wrong? Did Derek start another forest fire?" I asked, my fingers crossed.

"No. And he didn't start a forest fire. He was playing with matches in Jayden's backyard."

"It could've been serious," I said, solemnly. "Those poor squirrels without a home. Not to mention, coyotes hunting innocent children in the neighborhood."

"Oh, stop," my mother said. She sat down next to me. "I know you've been having some trouble with the Baby Bot, but I didn't realize how much. We got your progress report. You're failing science and home ec and health."

"I know," I said, disappointed. "It's not fair. I fell asleep during the science test. And the Baby Bot is just psycho."

To illustrate my point perfectly, Derek ran into the kitchen, holding his Baby Bot at arm's length. "Mom! This thing is psycho!"

The Devil Bot was fussing like no baby I had ever seen,

thrusting kicks and punches at Derek with reckless abandon. Derek took two uppercuts to the chin.

I laughed, and then prayed that his butt chin would swell up, so he could at least spend a few days understanding what it's like to not have the family butt chin, but my prayers were not answered.

To add insult to injury, Derek rushed to the table, hoping my mother would help. Without warning, his Baby Bot regurgitated its entire life's worth of food onto all three of us, which resulted in me having to get Baby Bot puke cut out of my hair. Having missing patches of hair was not in style at the moment. Nor should it ever be.

I WALKED into science class the next morning, sporting a black eye and a great haircut. I didn't know what to say to anyone.

Miss Kelvin rushed over to me. "Austin! Good news about your test."

My heart raced. Good news? I didn't know what to expect. "What is it?" I asked, excited.

"I was right about the score. You got a twelve."

"What's good about that?"

"Nothing. It's terrible. Even Flea beat that. I was just proud of my forecasting abilities."

I felt a lump in my throat. I almost couldn't speak. I felt tears well up in my eyes. "I'm really happy for you," I said, forcing a smile.

"You got five points for the DNA drool. I felt like that was generous," she said.

"Can I retake this? I wasn't feeling well, remember?"

"I'll talk to the chairman of the science department."

When I sat down, Flea looked at me and said, "A twelve? I've done worse, if that makes you feel any better."

"No. No, it doesn't."

"At least you didn't blow your eyebrows off this time."

"I didn't blow my eyebrows off. You did. And then you drew in new ones with a magic marker," I said, annoyed.

"I thought they looked good."

"No. No, they didn't."

Flea looked like he was going to cry.

"I'm sorry. I didn't mean to hurt your feelings. I'm just upset about getting a twelve on the test."

"I'm very self-conscious about my coloring ability."

Like I had time to deal with this...

The rest of the morning didn't get any better. By the time I got to Cherry Avenue, word was spreading about our Baby Bot run in. Supposedly, Ben had a concussion, Just Charles had internal bleeding, and Luke was in therapy. The third issue was probably true.

Sophie rushed up to me. "Are you okay?"

"I'm fine," I said.

"Nick DeRozan said you had a broken eye socket. Is the baby okay?"

"Spectacular," I said, sarcastically.

"Why didn't you tell me?" Sophie asked, annoyed.

"I didn't want you to worry."

She seemed annoyed at that, too.

"My brother was exaggerating, as usual," I said.

"Or you're not taking it seriously. As usual," Sophie said, before turning and walking away.

～

IN HEALTH and home ec class, Mrs. Flaum caught my eye as I entered the classroom. "Umm, Mr. Davenport. A word?"

"Okay," I said.

"And you, too, Miss Rodriguez," Mrs. Flaum said, pointing to Sophie.

Sophie furrowed her brow and joined me at the front of the classroom.

Mrs. Flaum studied our faces. "I checked your scores from the last week and saw some...interesting things going on with your baby."

"Is something wrong with our baby?" Sophie asked, horrified.

"You tell me," Mrs. Flaum said, simply.

Uh, oh. She was onto me. Sophie's eyes bore into me. The hack gone wack was about to back fire. Even more than it already did. On my face.

Mrs. Flaum continued, "Because I couldn't help but notice that your score was negative at one point."

"Negative?" Sophie asked.

"Well, most of the weekend."

"I think I know what you're talking about," I said, thinking as quickly as I could. "There was an incident that I didn't think babies were capable of." I looked at Sophie. "I didn't want to have to tell you this." I was hamming the drama up as best as I could. I looked at Mrs. Flaum and shook my head slowly. "I may have a defective baby. The software or something went crazy. I don't know that much about computers, well, software, but it seemed like it had a bug. Like a really big one. Or he's just really into mixed martial arts. But he's fine now."

I didn't want to look over at Sophie, but I did anyway. She did not look happy. I didn't know if I should keep going to try to make her happy or just shut my mouth and not make it worse. If you've heard any of my stories before, you've probably realized that I'm not very good at not making things worse. So, of course, I continued, "Okay. It was crazy. I almost ended up in the hospital. I thought I might have a broken jaw and a concussion. I'm thinking of taking legal action. The baby knocked four of us unconscious."

I looked back and forth between Sophie and Mrs. Flaum. The anger had turned to confusion. I was okay with that.

19

Sophie and I were in my basement, doing algebra together while the Baby Bot slept. Exciting stuff. But at least the baby was quiet.

"What did you get for number twelve?" Sophie asked, looking at her worksheet.

"Umm, X equals twenty-five lunatic Baby Bots," I said, laughing.

"I can't do this anymore," Sophie said, tossing her math book onto the couch.

"You like math," I said.

"I meant the baby."

"Oh. What can we do? It's hard."

"Our best. I need you to do your best. For me," she said.

"I'm trying. This thing is crazy," I said, pointing at Tre or Trevor or whatever it was that we named our Baby Bot.

"That's what I'm talking about," Sophie said, annoyed. "How can you call it 'this thing' and say you're taking it seriously? How can you learn to care for a baby when you don't treat it like a baby? You treat it like a doll you hate."

I nodded as I let Sophie's words soak in.

Sophie looked at her phone and said, "My mother's here. You need to think about it."

"Think about what?" I said, stupidly.

I followed Sophie, as she headed upstairs with the Baby Bot in its carrier.

"Honestly," she said. As we walked through the den, Sophie looked at my dad and said, "Thanks for having me over."

"Okay, Sophie. See you soon."

Sophie walked out the front door, without even a goodbye.

"Talk to you later?" I said.

"I'd rather you text to schedule your baby responsibilities."

"We can't talk?" I asked, confused.

"Why would we?"

"Because you're my girlfriend?"

"I'm not sure I want to be," Sophie said, disappointed. "In fact, I don't."

I watched her walk away in stunned silence.

Sophie settled into her mother's car and then disappeared down the street. I don't know how long I stood there, looking down the empty street. Mrs. Shikadance's dumb poodle's bark woke me from my stupor.

I walked back inside the house and to the den, plopping down next to my father.

"Everything okay?" he asked.

"No."

"What's wrong?"

"Sophie just dumped me. I don't get girls." I ran my fingers through my terrible hair and looked expectantly at my father, waiting for his words of wisdom.

All I got was, "Join the club, dude. Any particular

reason?"

"Sophie's all mad at me, because she says I don't take the whole Baby Bot thing seriously. It's an annoying robot. It's not a real baby. Kids are naming them. I think Sophie, Sammie, and Cheryl have started college savings plans. I don't get it."

"Well, get used to that," he said, again unhelpfully. "I see your point. It is just a robot doll. Or is it?"

"Huh?"

"There are very few hard truths in this world. A lot of it is how you look at things. Some kids are going all in, naming their babies, taking them for walks. Other kids, like you, see a stupid doll that screams all night. Who's right?"

"Me?"

My father laughed. "You're both right. But," he said, raising his finger in the air before continuing, "the objective of the assignment is to care for a baby. Yes, it's not real, but you are supposed to pretend it's real. Sophie's gone all in and is giving it her best. Are you?"

"I guess not," I said, defeated. "So, what should I do? How do I go all in? How do I get Sophie back?"

"That's for you to decide."

I lay down on the couch and stared at the ceiling, not having any idea what to do, my eyes tearing up.

Off in the distance, I heard my mother hurling. She had been sick for weeks. I was getting worried.

"Dad?"

"Yes, bud?"

I sat up and looked at him. "Is Mom dying?"

He chuckled. "No. She's not dying. She's just got a stomach bug or something."

"For weeks?"

"Sometimes, it takes a while for your system to handle these things."

"You sure?"

"Yes. So, what are you gonna do about Sophie and the baby?"

"I don't know," I said, collapsing back onto the couch. Wallow in self pity was the best idea I had at that moment.

THE NEXT DAY at school was a tough one. I was so tired, I could barely get off the bus. Barney had to escort me to science class.

He coached me as we walked. "Come on, buddy. You can do it. Just put one foot in front of the other. That's it. You got this, man. Lift, reach, plant. Lift, reach, plant."

I followed Barney's instructions as best as I could. I felt like I was in a movie during a slow-motion scene, but I knew it was nowhere near as cool. He led me into the classroom and over to my seat.

Barney continued, "Now, sit."

I plopped into my chair.

"Good, doggie," Barn Door joked.

I let out a bark for good measure.

Miss Kelvin looked at me, quizzically. "What's wrong, Austin?"

"I'm losing it, Ms. Kelvin. Or it may already be lost."

"Losing what?"

"All of it. My health. My dignity. My future. It's all going up in a cloud of baby fart."

"Huh?" She walked over to me, realizing I was in a world of hurt.

I continued, "I'm failing health and home ec. Plus, the twelve on my midterm. I've never failed anything in my life."

Flea said, "If I might add, you're also failing that haircut."

"Thank you, Flea, but I could use your support, not ridicule."

"Oh, I thought I was helping. You really should do something about that."

"Thanks, but I'm more concerned that I can't even make a cheeseburger. I keep burning them. Plus, I got dumped, and there's a fifty-fifty chance my mother is not going to make it through the year."

Ms. Kelvin's face registered shock. "Austin, are you serious? Is your mother okay?"

"My Dad said she'll be fine. Just a stomach bug. She keeps puking any time she sees raw meat and has these weird food cravings."

"Interesting," Ms. Kelvin said. "Well, I can probably help with the hamburgers. Cooking and baking are like science. You should be rocking the kitchen. You have to know your ingredients and how they react to heat and each other. It's no different than the elements. If you can excel here, you should be acing home ec."

Hmmm. I thought she could be right.

"I'll give you lessons," Flea said. "Just let me eat all the beef."

"Done," I said.

"Plus, I talked to the science chairman and he said we could waive your grade, but your final would count double."

"Really?" I jumped into her arms, excited.

Flea joined in, which added to the awkwardness.

When we parted, I said, "Sorry for the excitement. I needed this."

20

I was reinvigorated. Sophie was avoiding me, except for handoffs of the Baby Bot. So, I was focusing on other efforts. Flea was over at my place, taking up half the kitchen. And looking ever so tough wearing my mother's apron that said, 'Sassy Chick' with a picture of a baby chick giving some 'tude. The apron was stretched to its limits around Flea's oversized stomach.

Flea looked at me while forming a burger in his hands. "It all starts with the mindset. You must become one with the burger."

It sounded a bit out there, but I was willing to try anything to avoid failing.

My brother walked in and nearly fell over, his mouth dropping open.

"Can I help you?" I asked.

"Oh, well, I didn't know you had company." Derek looked up at Flea and said, "It's a real honor to meet you, Mr. Flea. I'm a big fan."

"Same here. Your brother told me you're a great football player."

"He did?" I asked, surprised. I wondered if I had a secret brother I didn't know about. Probably one with a butt chin. But then I realized Flea was talking about me, so I played along, saying more confidently, "Yeah, I mean, of course he did."

Flea said, "Keep up the good work. Maybe we'll play together some day."

"Looking forward to it!" Derek said, nearly skipping out of the kitchen and down the hall.

I hadn't seen Derek that dorked out maybe ever. His dream would probably come true sooner than expected given that Flea was likely to spend at least another few years in high school. He was on the ten-year plan, or so it seemed.

Back to burgers. I probably should've gone straight to the source, Burger Boys, and got a tutorial, because we spend so much money there. I'm sure they'd oblige. But this was a solid second option. Flea ate so much protein, seemingly in his quest to become The Hulk even when not angry, that he was the best person to teach me.

Flea continued, "Once you are one with the burger, you must have the appropriate lubrication." He sprayed the warming pan with cooking oil. "Two minutes on a side, medium heat should do it. If you had bacon in there, you could use that as extra lube."

"Bacon makes everything better," I said.

"That it does, little buddy. That it does." Flea handed me the spatula. "Why don't you flip it over?"

"Oh, I'm not sure."

"Just a little wrist twist," he said.

"I don't know," I said, staring at the burger.

"I'll show you," Flea said. He slid the spatula under the burger and took it out of the pan.

Leighton walked in behind us and said, "Hey, guys."

Flea turned around, the burger balancing on the spatula. When he saw Leighton, he panicked and tossed the burger into the air. It stuck to the ceiling with a thwack.

Flea's voice cracked as he asked, "What are you doing here?"

"I live here," Leighton said, simply.

"Right. What am I doing here?" Flea pondered the question. "For the life of me, I don't know."

We all just looked at each other and up at the burger on the ceiling, wondering what would happen next.

Flea seemingly calmed down and leaned up against the stove, casually. Well, he wasn't too casual for long.

He hopped up and shook his hands. "Ahhhh, farts," Flea said, trying to keep from crying. That was my line, but I wasn't going to tell him not to use it.

Leighton stepped forward. "Are you okay?"

"Perfect. I did that on purpose."

"You burned your hand in a frying pan on purpose?" Leighton said, frowning.

I quickly grabbed an ice pack from the freezer and handed it to Flea.

He applied it and said, "Yes. Yes, I did."

"Okay. I'm gonna go now," Leighton said, heading out of the room, confused.

I chimed in, "I think that's for the best." I looked at Flea once my sister left the room. "You okay, dude?"

"Yeah. I didn't know that was your sister. I kinda like her. I'm not good enough for her, though."

I didn't know what to say. He was kind of right in some ways. He wasn't the sharpest spatula in the drawer. But he had a big heart. And not just physically. He was a good dude. But I had enough on my plate, no pun intended, to worry about playing matchmaker. I was just glad that we had avoided another visit from the fire department. That's the last thing I needed.

Well, that and the burger that fell from the ceiling and landed on my head.

Just Charles arrived shortly after Flea left with news from the investigation on Randy's dinner guest at Burger Boys. I had given Just Charles the picture of the guy's license plate and let the master get to work. We settled in my room, needing to keep any sensitive material away from my brother, who would take pleasure in using it to his advantage or against me.

Just Charles dropped a folder on my desk. I flipped it open as he talked.

"I ran a nationwide search to find the license plate of Randy's visitor. I scoured emissions data and tracked it back to Wiley's Auto Body and Repair shop in Pleasantville."

"Nice work," I said. "Were you able to find out who owned the car?"

"Yep. The foolish mechanic emailed me the latest invoice. The car is registered to one Richard Langley."

I asked, "Do we know him?"

"I don't know anyone from Pleasantville," he said, shrugging.

"Yeah, that's far, isn't it?"

"Not far if you're a regional salesman."

"Will you stop with the dramatics and just tell me who he is?" I asked, shaking my head with a smile.

"Richard Langley is the regional salesman of Erudite Corporation, parent company of the Baby Bot 2000."

"Are you serious? So, what do you think Randy did?"

"I think he bought information from him. Maybe secret cheat codes," Just Charles said.

"I told you they existed! Exquisite work, my friend," I said, going in for a handshake, but missing.

"Now what?" Just Charles asked.

I tapped my chin as I thought. "How do we catch him? The sales guy will never tell. He'll lose his job. Randy won't give up the answers, either. Can we hack him?"

"To pieces?" Just Charles asked, horrified.

"No, his computer," I said, shaking my head.

"Maybe. Maybe we can get him to admit it. He's so arrogant, he probably thinks the rules don't apply to him."

"That he does," I said. "We need a plan."

There was a knock on my door.

"Come in," I called out.

The door opened, revealing a puffy-eyed Ben.

"What's the matter?" I asked.

"I got dumped," Ben muttered.

"Join the club," Just Charles said. He took a deep breath, seemingly trying to bury the still-raw emotions from Cheryl's dumping.

I asked, "What happened?"

Ben plopped onto my bed. "I was at Sammie's. She totally blindsided me."

"She's been dumping you for weeks," Just Charles said.

"Yeah, but the end. It was just so sudden."

"What did she say?" I asked.

"That I was too immature. That we wanted different things," Ben said, with a shrug.

"Like sushi?" I asked.

Ben nodded.

"Nobody's ever gotten dumped over sushi in the history of dating," Just Charles said, unhelpfully.

Ben hid his face in his hands.

"Good news," I said, trying to change the subject. "We've got the goods on Randy. Cheating. Again."

"What? Really?" Ben said, a little bit of energy returning.

"Should we call Luke?" Just Charles said, taking out his phone.

"Yes. We need to figure out how to trap Randy," I said.

"And Luke is gonna be the one to help us do that?" Ben asked.

I shrugged. "He's part of the team. Yeah, he might get benched sometimes, but he's on the squad."

Charles' phone rang on speaker.

Luke answered, "Yo! You're never gonna believe what happened! Dayna and I are going out!"

"What?" we all said in unison.

"We fell in love, caring for our Baby Bot together," Luke said, overly cheerful, at least for the mood our crowd was in.

"You guys left it outside half the time," I said, shocked.

Luke said, "Hey, man. Don't question Cupid. He knows what he's doing."

"Does he really?" Ben asked, annoyed.

"We're really happy for you," I said to Luke, rolling my eyes for the rest of us. "Meet us at Burger Boys. We have some work to do."

"Can't. Got a hot date. We're getting sushi!"

Ben snatched Just Charles' phone from his hand, hung up on Luke, and then tossed it onto the bed.

I WALKED into Burger Boys with Ben and Just Charles. My dad dropped us off to run some errands. It was mid-afternoon, so it was quiet. Dinner wouldn't kick in for two hours or so. The hostess looked up at us from the podium and asked, "Seating for three?"

"Please," I said. "I'd also like to speak to Lonnie, the manager."

The hostess' face dropped. "Is something wrong?"

"We need to report a crime," Ben said.

"Oh. Why don't you pick whatever booth you want and I'll go get him?" The hostess scurried away.

"Thanks," I said.

We slipped into the nearest booth and waited for Lonnie. It didn't take long. He hustled out, looking concerned.

"Austin. Boys. What's the matter? Wendy said something about a crime?"

"Yeah, it was a while back," I said.

"We did have a complaint about a patron peeing in one of the plants, but that's about it."

I rolled my eyes. "I wasn't peeing in the plant. I was just peering through it."

"*Right*," Ben said.

"Not helping, Benjamin." I looked up at Lonnie. "Here's the deal. That night, a most heinous crime took place and it wasn't in the plant. Randy Warblemacher bought cheat codes for a school project."

"Randy? What a nice kid. You ever see him throw a football? The kid has a big future ahead of him."

Things were not going smoothly.

"Yeah, spectacular," I said, unenthused. "Can we check the surveillance from that night with you?"

"Oh, I don't know. I'm not sure corporate would be happy about that," Lonnie said.

"Please. Please. Please. I'll get extra bacon on my burgers for the rest of my life. That will be like another ten grand in revenue for you," I said, my hands in prayer position.

"And you'll get nothing out of it?" Lonnie laughed.

"I didn't say that. Why can't this be a win-win situation?"

"I'd see if you want to work here, but I can't see you flipping burgers," Lonnie said.

I scoffed. "I can flip with the best of them," I said, lying. Well, perhaps stretching the truth. I hadn't practiced since my lessons with Flea. I looked at my crew and said, "Order me a Bacon Boy with extra bacon, and Lonnie and I will go check out the video."

"We're coming," Just Charles said, hopping out of the booth.

"Oh, all right," Lonnie said.

We followed Lonnie to the back, as we broke out into a chant of "Lon-nie rules! Lon-nie rules!"

We crammed into a small office behind the kitchen that smelled gloriously of bacon. Lonnie turned his computer screen toward us, as we stood behind his chair.

"Let's see what we got," he said, opening the security app.

"What was the date?" Lonnie asked.

"No idea," I said.

"Well, that kinda ruins things," Just Charles said.

Lonnie grabbed a stack of papers. "No worries! Somebody reported Austin's peeing incident." He rifled through the papers and said, "Ah, the 24th." He read the paper, "Nerdy kid peed in the tree next to the waitress station."

"That's ridiculous," I said.

"Well, you are nerdy," Just Charles said.

Lonnie scanned through the surveillance videos. "Do you know what time you were here?"

"About seven," I said.

Lonnie fast forwarded through a bunch of video.

"Hey, look! There's Austin peeing," Ben said.

"Peering! Not peeing!" I yelled.

Lonnie slowed down. "I stand corrected, Austin. There's definitely no peeing there."

"Can you get a different camera angle to see the tables on the other side of the waitress station?"

"I think I can do that," Lonnie said, clicking some buttons.

A perfect shot of the salesman, Randy, and Regan popped up on the screen, catching all of their faces. Randy even looked like he had buck teeth, which made it even better.

"Stop it there!" I said. "Can I have a printout of that?"

Lonnie clicked something and the printer began to whirl. "You didn't get this from me," he said.

21

We sat in Burger Boys and finished off the last few fries, waiting for my dad to return.

Just Charles slurped the final bit of his chocolate shake and asked, "Now what?"

"Baby Bonanza is only a few days away," I said.

"And our partners hate us," Ben added.

"If my analytical brain is correct, we all got dumped because the girls took the Baby Bots more seriously than we did," I said.

"I'm pretty sure I got dumped because of sushi," Ben said.

"Hibatchi I could see, but sushi?" Just Charles said.

"I love Hibatchi, guys, but back to my point. We can win the girls back by going all in." I told them about my conversation with my dad.

"How do we go all in? The Baby Bot experiment is over. And we failed," Just Charles said.

"No, it's not. First, we can crush Baby Bonanza, but second, I think we can do something special for them," I said.

"What?" Ben asked, excitedly.

I finished my French fry and said, "A shower."

"Dude, I shower every day *and* wear body spray," Just Charles said. "And I still got dumped."

"Do you think Sammie would find me more mature if I wore body spray?" Ben asked.

"No, but maybe if you wear *cologne*," Just Charles said. "And tell her you're shaving."

"Shaving what? His face is like a Baby Bot's butt. But I wasn't talking about that kind of shower. I was talking about a baby shower," I said, laughing.

Just Charles' eyes widened. "Do you think it could work?"

"What have we got to lose?" I asked.

WE HAD the $16 that I never paid my sister, which goes surprisingly far at the Dollar Store, and a plan. Well, we didn't have a plan yet, but we were working on it. We brainstormed as we stood on the checkout line at the store.

I held up a box. "I got cake mix."

"Can I hold it?" Just Charles asked, his eyes widening. He loved sweets and sugar. But when he had too much, he turned into Evil Chuck. You may remember him from some of my other stories.

"You're not going to be able to absorb the sugar through the box," I said, laughing.

"We need pizza," Ben said.

I shook my head. "I think it has to be sushi."

"Can we compromise with sushi on pizza?" Ben asked.

"That sounds like something Mrs. Zorch would do," Just Charles.

"Yeah, let's never mention that again," I said. "But let's have both. And maybe you could try a rainbow roll and see what you think."

"I think I might puke," Ben said.

"Well, you'll be in good company because all the Baby Bots, er babies, will be here," I said.

Just Charles scratched his head. "There is one slight problem. None of the girls are going to come over if we ask them."

I nodded. "Agreed, but we could get them over to Luke's house."

Ben looked re-energized. "We can have Dayna invite them over. She still probably doesn't remember any of our names."

"I think you're right," I said. "Let's get over there and get set up. We'll call Luke on the way."

WHEN WE GOT to Luke's, Dayna was already there with him. They led us into the kitchen, which would be our staging ground. I threw everything on the table.

I looked at Ben. "You and I will make the cake."

Just Charles whined, "Awww, man."

"Charles. Help the love birds decorate." I tossed him the bag of decorations. They landed on his foot. "Owww!"

I looked at Dayna. "Please invite Sophie, Sammie, and Cheryl over immediately. Don't tell them we're here."

"Okay," she said, but looked confused, as per usual. "But why would they care that you were here?"

"Right," I said. "They wouldn't." I rolled my eyes at Ben.

And then Ben and I got to work. Cracking eggs.

Measuring milk, cake mix, and oil. We whipped. We beated. We sweated. Mostly outside of the cake mix.

I set the oven and the timer, as Ben slid the cake into the oven, and then plopped into a kitchen chair.

"And now, we wait," I said.

"I don't have time to sit around. I never thought I'd say this, but I need to practice my swaddling," Ben said.

We walked into the den and grabbed a blanket from Lit Fart's diaper bag. I looked around the room for something to swaddle. I settled on a pillow and tossed it to Ben.

He laid the blanket out and placed the pillow inside.

And then I had a great idea. I walked into the dining room and asked Luke, "Do you still have all your sister's doll stuff?" She had like a hundred dolls with every outfit and accessory you could think of.

"Yeah, all that junk is down in the basement."

"Can we use it?"

"I don't care," he said.

I gave him a thumbs up and headed down to the basement. I made three trips back and forth, bringing dolls, diapers, blankets, and even a pair of crutches. I had no idea what I would use those for, but it pays to be prepared.

I returned to the den and laid out all the baby stuff I had gathered.

"If only Mr. Muscalini could see us now," Ben said.

I did my best Mr. Muscalini impersonation, "Sun's out, buns out!"

Ben followed, "Don't you know how to swaddle, Gordo? It's like rolling a burrito!" He then responded in his own voice, "Sir, I don't eat burritos!" And then back to Mr. Muscalini, "Good answer, Gordo! Burritos have carbs!"

And then we both froze. We heard the girls' voices in the foyer. Cheryl said, "What are you doing here?"

Just Charles stammered.

Ben and I headed out to meet them all. Sophie and Sammie looked at us, confused. Both of them held the Baby Bots.

"Hey," I said to Sophie.

"Hey," she said, monotone.

"What's going on?" Cheryl asked, annoyed.

I took a deep breath. "Well, we could tell you, but it's probably best if we showed you."

I wanted to take Sophie by the hand and lead her into the room, but I was too scared. So, I just did a tough guy and left her behind. I'm sure she thought it was cool.

We entered the dining room. There were decorations and party favors everywhere. A huge sign hung on the wall that read, 'Congrats on your baby shower!'

"What do you think? I may have erred on buying the noisemakers, but they were only a dollar," I said.

"You did all this?" Sophie asked, looking around in wonder.

"For you," I said, smiling. "And Trevor."

"Oh, Austin!" Sophie jumped into my arms and kissed me.

I nearly fell over. And not because she jumped into my arms. I looked over mid hug to see Ben and Just Charles getting similarly reunited. And apparently, Luke and Dayna didn't want to feel left out, so they started hugging, too.

"And there's cake!" Just Charles yelled.

"Yes. Let's not forget that's in the oven," I said to Sophie.

"Who would forget about something like that?" she laughed.

I shrugged. "Nobody I know."

"There's more," Ben said.

"Yes, there is. And now, for the icing on the cake," I said.

Just Charles' eyes lit up. "Icing?"

"Settle down, Charles," I said. "I give you our Baby Bonanza training facility." I led the crew into Luke's den, pointing at the dolls, diapers, blankets, and bottles we would use to change, swaddle, and feed those little bundles of joy better than Randy or Regan ever could.

"This is amazing!" Sammie said.

Sophie said, "We're gonna crush Randy."

"You have no idea," I said, smiling.

"What are you talking about?" Sophie asked.

I told the crew about Randy's picture and Just Charles' great work.

Cheryl looked at Just Charles and smiled. "Awwww, we could make such a great investigative team." Cheryl was the editor at the Gopher Gazette, our hard-hitting middle school newspaper.

"You're amazing," Sophie said.

"I know," I said, with a smile.

"Don't push it," she said.

"I always do."

22

W e had trained so much. I was so tired by the
time Friday morning rolled around, I didn't
know how I would be able to compete in the
Baby Bonanza. But then everything fell into place. And duct
tape was the key. Yep. You heard that right.

I walked into high school next to Barn Door. I heard
someone yell something that I had not heard in quite some
time. "Duct Tape Tornado!"

We hadn't had a duct tape attack in months, since I
glued those two kids and Principal Butt Hair to the floor.
Kids were diving left and right to avoid the storm that was
brewing. It was coming right at us.

Barn Door yelled, "Austin! No!"

But it was too late. And I didn't care. I let myself get
swept up into the storm, wrapped in layer after layer of duct
tape. I fell over onto the floor with a thud, but I barely felt it.

"Are you okay?" Barney asked.

"Totally fine. Just leave me, dude. I could use the rest."

"You sure?" he asked, surprised.

"A hundred percent."

"Okay," he said, not convinced. He walked away, watching me as he left.

I lay my head down on the floor. The cold floor, coupled with the feeling of security from the tight taping (some might even call it a duct tape swaddle), put me right to sleep.

Granted, Principal Butt Hair woke me up twenty minutes later and gave me a detention, but still it was the best sleep I'd ever had. I woke up refreshed and ready to rumble.

IT WAS FRIDAY NIGHT. Baby Bonanza had arrived. I looked around the room. I was prepared. I was energized. I was loaded with carbs. I figured Mr. Muscalini would at least be okay with carb loading on competition day.

I saw stations for diaper changes, swaddling, and folding laundry. There were rows of tables after tables lined up throughout the gym. It truly was going to be a Baby Bonanza. And then I threw up in my mouth. I saw the familiar face of none other than Calvin Conklin, the local doofus newscaster.

"Oh, God, no," I said.

"What's wrong?" Sophie asked.

I nodded my head at Calvin.

"Oh," she said. "He's not so bad."

"He's terrible," I said.

The participants sat down in the first few rows of the bleachers, holding our babies. A handful of teachers had volunteered to judge the contest. And of course, Ms. Armpit Hair was collecting money for her self-commissioned statue.

And then Calvin stepped forward with a microphone. He flipped his hair back and began. "Greetings, Gophers! As you already know, I'm the gifted newscaster from Channel Two!" There was a smattering of applause. And a few boos.

Calvin's face registered confusion. He tapped the microphone. "Is this thing on? Normally, women start fainting when I introduce myself." He looked around confused. "What am I doing here, anyway?" He pressed on his earpiece. "Ted, where am I? It looks like Zombie Fest. Not Zombie Fest? So, why does everybody look half dead here?"

We all just looked at each other, dumbfounded. I mean, we all knew Calvin was an idiot, but each time he hosted one of our events, somehow, we were all surprised when it bombed. Mr. Muscalini stood off to the side, shaking his head, as if he had been any better with the microphone at Zorch's wedding.

Mrs. Flaum walked up to Calvin and said, "Perhaps we can move on?"

"I guess," Calvin said, shrugging. "So, Ted tells me that we are here for Baby Bonanza! There will be twenty partners at each station and you will rotate when that enormous meat head back there blows his whistle."

Mr. Muscalini frowned.

"Why doesn't everyone go to their assigned stations so we can get this over with? I have a hot date." Calvin pressed on his earpiece again. "No, Ted. I won't shut up about my personal life. It's what endears me to the lowly public."

I carried Trevor to the diaper-changing station, Sophie right next to me. Calvin strolled through the crowd as everyone found their places. He strolled over to me, an eyebrow raised.

"Don't I know you?" Calvin asked.

"Maybe," I lied. I had so many run ins with Calvin over the past few years, I couldn't believe he wasn't certain who I was.

"Well, that's a precious little thing you have here," Calvin said, nodding at Trevor.

"Thank you," I said.

"He's got a butt chin, like me," Calvin said.

I took a deep breath. I had no interest in going there.

"Can I hold him?" Calvin asked.

I looked at Sophie, who shrugged. I said, "I guess so." I handed Trevor over.

Calvin cradled the baby in one arm and tickled his cheek. "Did anyone ever tell you that he looks like a robot?"

Sophie and I looked at each other and just chuckled.

Calvin leaned in and used his baby voice, "You're a wittle cutie. Tell me, what do you think of Uncle Calvin?"

I was about to tell Calvin that Trevor couldn't talk yet, but Trevor answered him just fine. Trevor's stomach rumbled and then regurgitated his dinner into Calvin's face with authority. So much came out of Trevor's mouth, pummeling Calvin, that he gasped for air, and I checked to see if Trevor was hooked up to some sort of never-ending puke hose.

I had never been prouder as a fake father.

Just as Trevor was finishing, Calvin apparently had had enough. He tossed Trevor in the air, and ran away, shrieking like a kid in a haunted house. As Calvin passed each Baby Bot, one by one, on his way to the exit, his shrieks set the Baby Bots off into hysterics, like they were car alarms after an earthquake. It was chaos.

But I didn't have time to worry about that. Trevor needed me. He was helicoptering through the gym, a solid ten feet away from me.

"Austin, save our baby!" Sophie yelled.

"I got this, baby! For real this time!" I yelled, surging toward Trevor with my hands outstretched.

I bumped into Curt Gentry and Macie Winthrop, and then slipped between them, my eyes locked on Trevor's falling plastic head. I reached out my hands, dove forward, and closed my eyes. My fingers felt the soft fabric of Trevor's onesie. I squeezed my hands shut, as I skidded to a squeaky and painful stop.

I looked around, holding Trevor. Sophie rushed over to me.

"You did it! Don't throw him again!"

We jumped up and down celebrating. I figured it would be okay since he had already regurgitated enough food for a week.

"This is crazy!" Ben said, rushing past us. "I've gotta get my boy outta here!"

I looked around. Babies were freaking out in every direction. Mr. Muscalini blew his whistle like he was trying to wake up the dead, but it only seemed to make things worse. Shocking, I know. And then Derek made things worse. Dozens of kids and screaming babies were jostling by the exit doors, trying to get away from the madness. Derek hopped out of the line and pulled the red fire alarm.

The fire alarm blared. The one Baby Bot out of the two hundred that wasn't crying, joined in.

Ms. Armpit Hair, Mr. Muscalini, Dr. Dinkledorf, and a few other teachers ushered the kids outside. By the time I got there, firetrucks and ambulances were pulling into the parking lot, sirens blaring.

As chaotic as it was, and frustrated that Trevor wasn't responding to the Bob and Shush, I was just glad that I wasn't the one who was responsible for the fire department showing up that night. It was all Trevor's fault. I guess the apple doesn't fall far from the tree.

"Let's get out of here and go to Frank's," I said, not wanting to see Officers Fontana and McGuire again.

"I'm in," Sophie said.

"Me, too," Ben said.

Just Charles looked at Cheryl. "We're in."

We all looked at Sammie, not sure what she would say. She smiled and gushed, "I could really go for some pizza. I miss it!"

We all cheered. Ben and Sammie hugged, which eventually turned into a giant, group hug.

And then my phone started to blow up. Not physically, although I could see how you might think that, given all the other mayhem I've told you about. I pulled my phone out of my pocket, still buzzing. I opened my Twitter app and raised an eyebrow as I read. My feed was ablaze with hashtags, links, and posts of jubilation.

"Guys, you're not gonna believe this," I said, a huge smile breaking out on my face.

"What is it?" Sophie asked.

Everyone gathered around to hear the news.

"The Baby Bot 2000 has been recalled!"

IT WAS the first time since I started health and home economics that I was excited to be there. I was on the edge of my seat, waiting for Mrs. Flaum to tell us what the whole Baby Bot recall meant.

Mrs. Flaum stepped forward. "Well, I had an interesting weekend, dealing with the whole Baby Bot recall," she said.

Everyone held their breath.

"We'll be sending them back immediately," Mrs. Flaum said.

There were a few whispers. I didn't know what to say.

"What does it mean for our grades?" Sophie asked.

"I talked it over with Ms. Pierre and the only thing to do is to give everyone As!"

The class broke out into hysterics. We all jumped up and cheered. Kids were hugging other kids they had never even spoken to. Ever. Nerds high-fived athletes. We didn't connect on all of them, but still, there was harmony between the two enemy groups for the first time in a long time.

I hugged Sophie, and then Ben and Sammie. When I let go of the two of them, I turned around, looking for someone else to hug. I looked up at none other than Randy Warblemacher. There was no way I was hugging that kid, but I took a deep breath, swallowed my pride and held out my hand for a shake.

Randy looked down at my hand, smirked, and then turned his back on me.

I chuckled to myself and shook my head.

In the chaos, I walked over to my desk, slipped a manila envelope out of my backpack, and dropped it onto Mrs. Flaum's desk. When the dust settled from the celebration, she walked back to her desk and sat down. She frowned as she picked up the envelope.

"That's funny," she said. "I didn't notice this before." She opened the envelope and slipped the picture of Randy, Regan, and the Baby Bot sales guy out of it. "Hmm, that's Richard. He's the regional salesman for the Baby Bot 2000." She looked over at Randy and Regan. "Why is there a picture of you having dinner with him?"

Randy and Regan looked at each other, both of their faces morphing pale.

Randy said, "He sat down at the wrong table!" while Regan said at the same time, "He's my uncle!"

"Looks like you have some explaining to do," Mrs. Flaum said. "I'll get someone to watch the class. Let's head down to Ms. Pierre's office, shall we?"

The class let out a collective, "Ooooooh."

Randy and Regan stood up, and followed Mrs. Flaum, no smirks to be found on either of their faces.

I looked at my crew. I didn't know what the opposite of "Aaaaahhh, farts!" was, but my smile said it all.

It was a fabulous day. Even the seafood surprise tasted better that day.

23

A fter school, I stood in the Atrium with Sophie, who was holding Trevor in her arms. Half of the eighth grade was lined up. Jimmy Trugman and Ellie Germano were in front of us. They handed in their baby and walked away. It was our turn. I stepped forward. Sophie handed me Trevor and ran away, crying.

I called out, "Sophie, wait!" But it was too late.

"Are you ready?" Mrs. Flaum said.

"Yep." I looked down at Trevor and said, "We didn't always see eye to eye, son. But you taught me how to go all in. And for that, I'm grateful. True, my parents are going to have to spend thousands for therapy because of you, but still, it was an important lesson. I hope that with a software upgrade, you won't be such a lunatic." I looked at Mrs. Flaum. "I guess that's it. This is goodbye."

"Maybe you can spend some time with him over the summer after his, umm, treatment," Mrs. Flaum suggested.

"Umm, no. I think it's best we make a clean break," I said. "But I assure you, I will never forget Trevor here."

I HAD NEVER FELT SO relieved. We sat around the dinner table, my entire family there. Fried chicken and mashed potatoes. Another one of my mother's weird cravings.

"Well, congratulations are in order, I guess?" my dad said. "You survived."

"Thanks," I said. "I'm never having kids. I don't even want to see another baby ever in the history of my life."

Derek added, "I agree. And while we're at it, can we get rid of Austin, too? He's still the baby of the family."

"This is lovely," my mother said, sarcastically. "Your father and I have some news for you all."

"We're getting a trampoline?" Derek asked.

"A puppy?" Leighton asked.

My mother said simply, "Austin's *not* the baby in the family anymore."

"What?" we all yelled in unison.

"Your father and I are pregnant!"

"Dad, you are looking a little thick in the waist," Derek said.

"Very funny."

"Wait, what?" I asked.

"We're having a baby!" my mother said, excitedly.

Derek put his hands together in prayer position. "I hope he has the butt chin. I hope he has the butt chin."

"We don't know what we're having. We're going to a sonogram to find out soon. Do you guys want to come?" my mother asked, excitedly.

MY WHOLE FAMILY sat in the exam room at the doctor's office.

My dad held my mother's hand while a man in blue scrubs readied a sonogram sensor for my mother's belly. The technician squeezed a tube of gel onto my mother's belly and said, "It's gonna be cold."

"I remember. This is number four for me."

"Do you want to know the baby's gender or do you want to do a big reveal?"

"No, let's do it here," my mother said.

The technician held the sensor on my mother's stomach and moved it around. He whispered, "What the- Oh, my God!"

"What is it?" my mom asked, concerned.

My heart started to race. I wasn't sure if the baby was okay.

"I've never seen anything that big before," the technician said, shaking his head.

"So, it's a boy?" my dad asked, wide-eyed.

"No, it's a girl. That chin. It's a huge butt. It's bigger than the baby's real butt!"

Ahhh, farts!

COMING SOON

September 15th, 2020

November 15th, 2020

Got Audio?

Want to listen to Middle School Mayhem?

ABOUT THE AUTHOR

C.T. Walsh is the author of the Middle School Mayhem Series, set to be a total twelve hilarious adventures of Austin Davenport and his friends.

Besides writing fun, snarky humor and the occasionally-frequent fart joke, C.T. loves spending time with his family, coaching his kids' various sports, and successfully turning seemingly unsandwichable things into spectacular sand-wiches, while also claiming that he never eats carbs. He assures you, it's not easy to do. C.T. knows what you're think-ing: this guy sounds complex, a little bit mysterious, and maybe even dashingly handsome, if you haven't been to the optometrist in a while. And you might be right.

C.T. finds it weird to write about himself in the third person, so he is going to stop doing that now.

You can learn more about C.T. (oops) at ctwalsh.fun

 facebook.com/ctwalshauthor

ALSO BY C.T. WALSH

Down with the Dance: Book One

Santukkah!: Book Two

The Science (Un)Fair: Book Three

Battle of the Bands: Book Four

Medieval Mayhem: Book Five

The Takedown: Book Six

Valentine's Duh: Book Seven

The Comic Con: Book Eight

Election Misdirection: Book Nine

The 250-Year-Old Bride

The Kung Pao Cow

Future Release schedule

Class Tripped: September 15th, 2020

Graduation Detonation: November 15th, 2020

CPSIA information can be obtained
at www.ICGtesting.com
Printed in the USA
BVHW041924150920
588872BV00022B/410